VICTORIA ASHLEY

WALK OF SHAME #2

HEMY
Copyright © 2014 Victoria Ashley
All rights reserved.

Cover by CT Cover Creations
Stock photo ©123RF.com
Edited by Charisse Spiers
Interior Formatting and Design by Christine Borgford, Perfectly Publishable

PROLOGUE
Hemy

I FEEL A HAND ON my shoulder pushing and shaking me, causing me to groan and scratch my head. I'm so fucked up that I can barely even move. To be honest, this could just be my mind screwing with me again, so I choose to ignore it.

"Dude. Hemy. Get the hell up. Wake up, bro."

I make an attempt to open my eyes, but all they do is end up rolling into the back of my head and closing. I'm in the middle of my drug-induced coma, fucked out of my mind. My eyes are so heavy that I don't even bother trying to open them again. All I want to do is sleep, to not have to think. My mind is a fog, no clues as to where it's been or what it's done in the past twenty-four hours; my synthetic nirvana.

"It's time for you to get out, man. Take Rachel and go. I got shit to do." The voice echoes through my ears, not sticking to my mind for shit except for one word.

All it takes is Rachel's name for my mind to register what the hell is going on and for me to sober up enough to move. I knew I shouldn't have come here last night. All I wanted was a quick release from my hell for ten minutes. I didn't expect to get as trashed as I did, but then again I never do until it's too late.

Sitting straight up I open my eyes and shake my head, as if that's going to take me out of the state I'm in. The room starts spinning around me, so I lean forward with my head in my hands and squeeze my eyes shut. I need to come down, but my mind is still off in the land of the thoroughly fucked up.

"Dude . . . I told you to take it easy last night, but you were unstoppable as usual."

My brain finally starts to process and I open my eyes again to see my good friend, Mitch, standing above me with my shirt in his hands. He looks both pissed off and sorry for me at the same damn time.

He throws my shirt at my face and it ends up landing on my lap, which I just now realize is covered with Rachel's face buried in the middle. Rachel groans and digs her face into my hard on, but doesn't wake up.

Damn.

In one quick movement I push Rachel out of my lap and jump to my feet. "Ah, fuck." I rub my hands over my face and step away from the bed. "What is this shit?"

Rachel opens her eyes and smiles seductively while reaching for my pant leg. I shake her hand off and push it away. "What's wrong, baby? You seemed to be into me last night. Did I do something wrong?" She pokes her bottom lip out in a pout.

Pointing my finger in her face I take a deep breath and exhale, trying to keep my anger in check. "The fuck I was. You know damn well I don't want shit to do with you." I grab for my shirt and start backing away. "I'll deal with your ass later. I told you this shit had to stop. I have to go."

I rush through the house with Mitch trailing closely at my heels. As soon as I push my way outside, I stop and take a few deep breaths in an attempt to gather myself from the shit storm I just walked out of. My head is spinning even faster now, and I have no idea how I'm going to get my ass home in this condition. I can barely even stand up straight.

"I have some bad news, bro." Mitch's voice is soft and full of regret coming from beside me.

I don't like the sound of this. I lean against the brick wall of the house and rub my hands over my face as fast as I can. "Just say it, man."

Mitch leans against the wall beside me. He hesitates for a short moment, meaning he doesn't want to say what it is he has to tell me. "Onyx came over looking for you this morning. I tried telling her that you weren't here, but man, she isn't stupid."

I turn around and pound my fist into the brick wall as hard as I can, repetitively, angry with my damn self. The crackling of bone against the wall tells me how much pressure I'm exerting behind each swing. The drugs swarming through my bloodstream numbs my mind from the pain I would be experiencing otherwise. "What did she see," I ask through gritted teeth. "Why didn't you wake me up? Fuck, I could have explained everything."

"I tried waking your ass up. You were too fucked up. She walked in the bedroom and saw you shirtless with Rachel laying across your lap. She just stood there motionless for a while before turning around and walking out. She seemed pretty calm, man. I don't know. I tried explaining, but she just kept walking, mumbling something about eternal heartache."

I let out a huff and glide my fingers through my sweaty hair. "How the hell did Rachel get in there with me? When I went to that room last night I was alone. I didn't do shit with her. I never once touched her." My jaw steels as I picture Rachel's scheming hands on me. This isn't the first time she has pulled this shit.

"I don't know, dude. I just went in there this morning to make sure your ass was still *breathing* and there she was, half naked, and sleeping on your lap. I didn't know what the hell happened, so I just left you two alone." He throws his arms up to show me he doesn't really want to get involved. "I'm sorry, man. I think your time with Onyx is up. Everyone has a breaking point, a moment when they throw in the towel and walk away. You've screwed things up way too many times. You need to get your shit together before you end up dead and alone."

I stand here and let his words sink in as he pushes away from the wall and walks away, ending the conversation. I'm at a loss for words. I know I'm nothing but a big fuck up. I've always been worthless. Even my parents thought so.

Giving my body a few more minutes to wake up and get with the program, I just stand here with my eyes closed, gripping the wall in front of me. I can feel the blood starting to ooze out of the torn skin, running down my fingers, but only because of the wetness and not the pain. I'm still numb from the pain, I always am. It's what I spend all of my time chasing, and the reason I'm in this situation. How the hell am I going to explain this shit to Onyx? She'll probably be gone by the time I get there.

Dammit, I fucked up . . .

THIRTY MINUTES LATER I PULL up in front of my apartment and hop off my motorcycle. It took me that *long* to be able to somewhat function normally. Even from the street I can see a couple of her suitcases on the porch, telling me what a damn screw up I am.

I stand here watching Onyx as she throws another bag out onto the porch, not even bothering to look my direction. It's really happening. She's really leaving and I am too fucked up to even fight for her. I am barely holding the bile down that is rising in my throat. Even I think I'm a loser at the moment. How am I supposed to convince her otherwise?

Setting my helmet down on my seat, I sprint over to the porch and reach for her arm just as she sets down another bag. "It wasn't what it looked like. Let me explain."

Her scorching green eyes meet my amber ones and I feel my heart drop to my stomach. There is nothing left in her look but hatred and pain, and it hurts even more knowing where it came from. I did this to her and I've been doing it for the last six years.

"It doesn't matter, Hemy," she mutters. "You don't think I know you didn't sleep with that tramp? I know it . . . but the question is how much did she enjoy getting off on you while you were drunk, high, and passed out? How do you expect me to feel about all of this, huh? The thought of her touching you makes me want to puke. Her hands groping your body, touching your hair; being places mine should be. I can't do it anymore, I can't continue to stay in the shadows, tormenting myself mentally over you. I just can't."

I swallow and place my hand on her chin, stepping closer to her. I see her eyes dart down to my lips before she pulls her face away and takes a step back. "Don't," she whispers. "Just. Don't. Please, let me go."

It hurts having her push me away. Not being able to touch my woman is the worst pain ever, but I don't blame her. "I have no excuse. I'm a mess. I know that. I'm trying to get by the only way I know how, which is to forget sometimes."

"Well, I can't take it anymore. I just can't deal with it. I gave it everything I had, and now there is nothing left to give. Every day that I'm with you I die a little more inside; lose a little more hope. I understand that you had a messed up childhood. I understand that your shitty parents left you. You were a young child, alone, and scared out in the world; I get that, and I can't tell you that your sister is still out there, or that she is even still alive. I can't take that all back, but what I can do is show you that love exists, that I'm always here for you. I have tried. I really have, but I can only take so much, Hemy. I understand your reasoning behind your behavior, but at the end of the day . . . I should be your only." Her voice is broken and it kills me.

She breaks down in tears while moving further away from me as if being close hurts too much. I have the urge to run my hands though her strawberry curls and hold her close, but I don't. I can't. I don't deserve to. "You're a lost cause, Hemy. I can't force you to change. You can't and won't. I'm only eighteen, dammit . . . and you're only nineteen. This is all too much to handle. We're too young for this shit. Can't you see that?"

"I can change. I just need time. My head is not in a good place and I'm not strong enough to move on just yet. Do you know how hard it is to wake up every morning with these memories?" I point to my head, my hand shaking. "The places I have been. The people I have seen. The things I saw my parents do to Sage. It's a gaping wound on my brain. Now I don't even know where the hell she is! She was only nine at the time. I was supposed to protect her. I'm trying my best here, okay?"

"I'm sorry," she whispers. "I tried to help you. I tried, but I can't continue to immerse myself into this filth and heartache. You may not have touched her this time, but what about next time? What extent will you go to in order to get your way of forgetting, huh? I have to get out of here before I lose myself." Her eyes meet mine and her bottom lip quivers. "I've already lost *you*, because you were never fully there to begin with. I have known you for six years; for six years, Hemy, and you have only gotten worse. Don't turn into your parents. Don't let them win."

I turn away from her, no longer able to look at the disappointment in her eyes. It hurts too damn much. "Can you just give me one more chance? I promise I would never hurt you on purpose. The things you've seen in the past were beyond my control. I may have flirted a little when I was high out of my mind, but I have never taken another woman to bed."

"From what you know of, Hemy," she bites out in a clipped tone. "We don't know that for sure and I'm not sticking around to find out. I have to go. I *need* to go. You've hurt me too many times and I feel as if I can't breathe anymore. It. Hurts. So. Much."

She turns around and heads for the door, but then stops. "I just have one question. Have you ever loved me?"

Her words linger in the air as I try to force myself to speak. I want to say yes, but the truth is, I'm not sure I know what love truly is. "Onyx, I-"

"No. No. No. I don't want to hear any excuses. I get it." She grips the doorframe, but doesn't turn to face me. "Tell me you love me, Hemy. Give me some kind of hope, because I've lost it all."

My heart speeds up and it becomes hard to breathe. I'm not worth it and we both know it. She said it earlier when she said I was a lost cause. "I'm sorry," is all I can manage to get out. Someone of my caliber doesn't know how to love. It isn't in my genetic makeup. As bad as I want to keep her here, she deserves so much better. But I'm selfish when it comes to her.

Without turning back she lets out a soft cry and covers her mouth. "Don't bother contacting me, Hemy. I'm moving away from Chicago and I have already changed my number. There's nothing more to be said between the two of us."

"Don't say that," I whisper. "I can't fucking lose you too."

"It's too late. You already have." She bends down and reaches for one of her bags, and that's when I notice her brother outside tossing her bags into his trunk. "My family has already been instructed not to

10

tell you where I'm going. You won't be able to change their minds, so don't try. Goodbye, Hemy. It was fun while it lasted, right?" She laughs sardonically. "Have a nice life."

I fall against the back wall while letting her harsh words sink in. My hands reach up to cover my face and my heart feels as if it's been ripped from my chest; I'm no longer breathing.

The longer I stand here without her the more it hurts; the more I feel like dying. *What the hell am I doing?*

"No, wait!" I run to the door and open it, but I'm too late. She's already gone. I quickly search for my phone, but of course I am so damn stupid that I must have lost it last night.

I turn around and reach for the closest thing to me, slamming it down next to my feet before punching a hole through the wall. What's a few more breaks or scratches going to hurt? Maybe the physical pain in my hands will take away from the pain that is now throbbing in my chest. Trying to catch my breath, I fall against the wall behind me and drag my back down it until I'm on the floor burying my hands in the thickness of my hair.

So this is what love truly feels like . . . and losing it hurts like a bitch.

CHAPTER
ONE
Hemy

Four years later . . .
THE AIR AROUND ME SMELLS of booze, sex, and drugs, my usual Saturday night scene. At one point I lived for these wild nights that consist of bodies upon bodies of people just looking to let loose, get fucked up, and fucked hard without the harsh judgments of society. It became my life; my very reason to breathe . . . until it *fucked* my life up. Then it became my ruin.

I'm leaning against the wall, casually chillin' in the shadows while slamming back a bottle of Whiskey. Lurking in the darkness is the person I've become. I've been at it for the last hour. This party is piled high with willing pussy and roaming hands, yet I've let my thoughts pull me under and drown me in my own fucked up world of mistakes and regret. Tonight, I may need a bit of a challenge to get me off. I'm going to need it rough, deep and fast.

While slamming back another drink of Whiskey my eyes stray over to a petite brunette; Nico's new girl. I met Nico a few years ago at one of these parties while I was high out of my mind. We partied together and we slowly became friends. I like him because he's just as fucked up and twisted as I am.

Nico's girl is slowly swaying her hips to a seductive song while rubbing her ass all over his dick. Her eyes are glued to me, eyeing me up and down like a siren luring her next victim. Fucking perfect. I like the seductress types, because they usually like the rough and rowdy sex that I require. The more she dances the more erotic her moves become. She's working it well, because I feel my feet moving in her direction, not thinking of anything but giving her what she wants. It's a nice distraction.

Nico's lost in his own little world, grinding himself on her backside, but he stops to tilt back a drink of beer and takes notice of me approaching. He watches me with satisfaction; his eyes say it all. A cocky smirk takes over his lips as he gives me a head nod and steps aside. He knows exactly what's coming, and he welcomes it. "Hey, man." He gives me a fist pound before practically pushing his woman into my arms. "Take care of Peyton for me. I know you'll treat her right, man." Most men don't want to share once they've claimed a pussy, but Nico thrives on it. I told you he is just as fucked up as I am.

I grab his girl by the hip and pull her flush against my body. Grinding my hips in rhythm of the music, I press her against the wall and brush my tongue over her lips, causing her to moan out and wrap her arms around me. Our bodies press into each other's as I lean in to whisper in her ear. "You've been watching me all night." I press my body a little closer to hers and tug her hair a little. "Are you sure you can handle me once you get me? I'm not so sure Nico has told you about me. I don't fuck like a boy I fuck like a man. I like it wild, wet, rough, and rowdy. If you want a lover this is your chance to back out. "

She sucks in her bottom lip before turning to Nico who is now standing right next to us with a smile on his face. "So this is Hemy, huh?" She gives me a look of approval before letting out a growl and leaning over to bite Nico's lip. "I can definitely get down with this, baby. Are you sure?"

Nico nods while tilting back another drink of beer.

Don't ask me why, but Nico has this weird shit of getting off to me fucking his girls. It's like it turns him on to know that I've been inside them. It could always be that he just enjoys the show. Either way, I'm not complaining.

I slide one hand up her skirt to grip her tight little ass while running my lips up her neck. "You want me to take you upstairs and fuck you? I bet you're already wet for me." She nods her head and plays with the top button of my shirt while biting her lip with need. "Has Nico told you the filthy things I do, because I'm not one to take it easy? Once I'm inside you, it's deep and hard. There's no in between, sweetheart."

She reaches up to grip my hair as Nico pushes behind her with his body and wraps one of her legs around my waist. He grips her thigh and bites her neck. The way that he's grinding his hips is causing her pussy to rub against my erection, which makes me want to fuck right here in this crowded room; it

14

wouldn't be the first time. "This is so hot right now," she breathes. "I'm ready for this." She lets out a satisfied moan and leans her head back and turns it to the side so that Nico can crush his lips against hers.

Ignoring everyone around us, I lace my hand in the back of her hair and run my tongue over her neck as she grinds into me while kissing Nico. I pull away from her neck and run my tongue over my bottom lip. "Are you sure you can handle me giving your girl a good fuck, Nico? I have some pent up shit to get out. I'm not playing it fucking nice tonight."

"Mmm." He releases the lock their lips have been in, and nods his head. Grasping the top of her head, he pulls downward, revealing her neck closer to his lips for access. "I need this shit tonight. We both want it and you know damn well that you do too," he says with a cocked eyebrow. "Don't back out on me, Hemy."

I smirk as Nico runs his tongue along her jugular and steps back, pushing his hair out of his face. "You know I'm down. Just giving your ass a warning."

With force, I grip Peyton's thighs and pick her up to wrap her legs around my hips. Immediately, she locks them around my waist. The lust in her eyes is thick. No matter the girl, they all have a wild side waiting to be released.

I turn back to Nico while gripping Peyton's ass and sliding one hand under her short dress. There is nothing but a thin string between her pussy and my fingers. I can feel her wetness coating me as she moves back and forth, swaying her hips against me. "You ready to watch Peyton's pretty little pussy get fucked?"

Nico watches me as I push my way through the crowd with his girl plastered to my front. He usually gives me time alone first before he joins in. It's a little routine that he has developed since we started this.

Sucking on Peyton's bottom lip I make my way up the stairs and to the nearest empty room. Turning the knob with my free hand I push the door open with my knee and toss her down onto the bed in front of us.

With her hands gripping the blanket, she spreads out on her back, her eyes locked with mine. Her breathing is out of control with need. "I've never done anything like this before." She runs her tongue over her lips and backs up against the headboard. "I want to. I do. I'm a little nervous though."

Yanking my shirt over my head I walk over to the foot of the bed and grip her thighs while crawling onto the bed above her. Her eyes widen as they take in my build. "Don't be nervous. I want to fuck you and he wants to see it. There's no shame in that." Gripping her thighs tighter, I spread her legs wide for me and pull her up to meet my hips with a smirk. "I hope you like it long and deep, because that's all I can give you."

Before she can respond I have her dress above her head, ripping it away from her body. My eyes trail over her toned form, admiring it for a moment. "Damn, girl." I pull her up, so that she's straddling my lap as I grind my cock against her swollen clit. Her underwear are already moist, just the way I expect them to be.

Her hands reach out to grip my hair as she rocks back and forth, enjoying the feel of my body against hers. "You're so sexy," she whispers. "I can see why Nico gets off to this shit. It's a little different, but it's the hottest thing I've ever done."

Sitting up on my knees, I arch her back and run my lips over her stomach, stopping at her breasts. "Oh yeah? You like this?" Reaching behind her with one hand, I grip the thin fabric of her bra and rip it open. Her eyes watch me with need as I run my other hand up her stomach before pushing her bra out of the way.

My lips come down to meet her right nipple, gently at first, before I tug on it with my teeth. They are puckered, revealing just how turned on she is. A moan escapes her lips as she rocks her hips into me again, causing me to run my tongue over her soft flesh and growl. "Hemy," she breathes, "I want your cock inside me."

I strain my eyes to look up at her, but keep her nipple in my mouth, sucking the pebble gently and then hard, as I slide my hand down the front of her thong. I glide my finger up and down her wetness before burying it deep inside her tight little pussy.

Her breathing picks up as her hands dive into my long hair, tugging and tangling with deep pants. "Oohhh, that feels so good. Don't stop." Her eyes close as I run my tongue along her smooth body, moving from one breast to the other, all while working my finger deep inside her. I can feel her wetness start to drip down my hand as her body starts to shake in my arms.

"Not yet," I demand. "Save it for Nico." I slow my movement, knowing that at any second Nico will be arriving. She's too preoccupied to take notice, but I hear the footsteps down the hallway getting closer with each passing second. I want him to watch her come under my touch. It's pleasurable for all of us. He likes being the audience and I like being the actor; she gets a good fuck out of it. Everyone wins.

I tilt my head to the side and smirk as Nico steps into the room. *Perfect timing.* Grinding my hard cock underneath her body, I shove another finger inside her and start fucking her hard and fast while biting on her nipple.

"Shit! Oh fuck! That's it, right there . . . . yeah." Her screams come out with a moan as her orgasm takes over, her body clenching my fingers upon her release. "Hemy," she breathes. "Don't stop. I need more." I always did favor a vocal woman in the bedroom, one that tells me exactly what she wants.

I grab her face and turn it to face Nico. Her breathing picks up as he leans against the door watching us. She's starting to feel the high that Nico gets a rush on. It's easier to digest when you realize it's no different than watching a porno, only in real life. Then it doesn't seem so twisted to the outside looking in.

"Take a seat, Nico." I run my tongue up Peyton's lips while pulling my finger out of her pussy. "Things are just heating up. I hope you're ready."

Without waiting for a response I grip her panties in my hands and quickly pull them down her slender legs. I toss them toward Nico and see them land on the arm of the chair he is now sitting in.

Peyton takes turns looking between me and Nico while breathing heavily. She wants to be sure he's watching, silently awaiting his approval to continue. The thought of knowing he's there turns her on. It turns me on.

Standing up from the bed, I pull her by her ankles, aligning her ass with the edge of the bed. I grab both of

Peyton's hands and place them on my belt as she sits up. "Take it off. Everything."

Her hands work fast to undo my belt before she goes for my button and zipper. Within five seconds, my jeans are being pushed down my thighs and I'm quickly kicking them out of the way.

"Have you ever had a pierced cock inside of you before?" She shakes her head as her eyes look downward toward my erection. "Good. Take my briefs off, Peyton. Show Nico how hard I am for you."

She glances over at Nico before biting her bottom lip and slowly pulling my briefs down. My cock springs free from the material, getting a small gasp from Peyton. I can't tell if she's excited or terrified by its size, not to mention the two steel bars pierced through it. This girl is in for something she never saw coming.

"You like my cock, Peyton?" She nods her head. "Taste it. Rub your sweet little tongue over it. Bite it, suck it, and make it yours." I tangle my fingers into the back of her hair while pushing her head down to my cock. The thought of her boyfriend watching her take in my thick cock only makes me harder; making me want to fuck her mouth even faster and deeper.

Her tongue darts out to swirl around the head of my cock before she suctions the top of it into her mouth. She has to open her mouth extra wide to take in its thickness.

I turn to the side and grip her hair harder while giving Nico a view of me fucking his woman's mouth. His eyes meet mine for a brief second before moving down to my length that is barely even half way in Peyton's mouth. I thrust in and out, grinding my hips while pulling on her hair. I can see Nico's cock grow hard through his jeans as he takes in a deep breath and exhales.

"Touch it," I demand. "Pull out your cock and stroke it while I fuck her mouth. Pretend her lips are on *your* dick, sucking it, licking it, and making it come. Show her how good it makes you feel."

His eyes darken with desire as he shoves his hand down the front of his jeans and starts stroking himself with a loud moan. He's slowly working himself up to join.

"Peyton," I whisper. "Stand up."

She runs her hand up and down my shaft a few more times before pulling her mouth away and doing what she's told. Her tongue runs over her mouth, tasting me on her lips before she looks behind me at Nico.

"Grab my hair and hold the fuck on," I growl, "And you better fucking watch, Nico."

Her hands reach out and grip my hair as I lift her up so that she is sitting spread eagle on top of my shoulders, her pussy in my face. I walk over to the wall next to Nico and press Peyton's back against it, hard. I want to be sure he can see *everything* I'm about to do to her body. I look up at her. "Hold on tight and don't let go."

Once she has a good grip on my hair, I spread her pussy lips and run the tip of my tongue over her clit. I feel her body tremble from my touch, so I softly suck it into my mouth while shoving a finger inside of her, fucking her soft and slow to loosen her up for what's to fill her later.

From the corner of my eye, I see Nico undo the button of his jeans before leaning back in his chair and gripping his hair. "That's so damn hot. Yeah. Finger fuck her tight little pussy."

I devour her pussy even harder as I reach up with one hand and grip her breast in my hand, squeezing it until I hear her moan out. Her moans turn to screams as I suck her clit harder into my mouth in rotation with running my tongue up and down her wetness and moving my finger in and out in perfect rhythm.

I hear the sound of Nico's zipper before I see his cock break free from his boxers from my peripheral vision. He's stroking his cock with one hand while gripping the arm of the chair with his other. He's so turned on that he doesn't know what to do with himself. He can't even sit still. I don't blame him. Seeing me fuck Peyton with my tongue has to be a damn hot sight. I know I'm good at pleasuring anyone I get my hands on; eating pussy is my specialty.

I look up at Peyton while circling my tongue over her swollen clit. "You ready to come again? Then, when you're done, I'll bury my cock deep inside of you."

She leans her head back and tries to keep her leg from shaking. Her thighs are practically squeezing my head off, but I keep spreading them wide so Nico can see my tongue on her soft pink flesh.

"Yes." She nods her head while moaning. "Yes. This feels so good. So good."

I smile against her pussy before pulling away from the wall and kneeling on my knees, setting her down on the plush carpet close to where Nico is sitting with his cock in his hand. "Turn over and get on your knees." I rest on my knees and stroke my hard cock while waiting for her to get positioned. "Such a hot little pussy, Nico. Thanks for letting me get a taste."

I run my hand down the seam of her spine and down the crack of her ass until I reach her wet pussy. Spreading her wide, I bend forward until my tongue is aligned over her pussy, plunging it inward. I fuck her with my tongue and run the thumb of my free hand over the puckered hole above, causing her to tense; the reaction I was looking for. I like a little anal play from time to time, and the girls love the sensation mixed with filling their pussy.

Her hands grip the carpet as she moans out. "I'm about to come. I'm so close." I speed up, shoving my tongue deeper while messaging the opening to her ass above. "Yes! Right there. Ahhhh!"

Her body trembles beneath me and I have to catch her to keep her from falling over. I can hear Nico's breathing pick up as his strokes become longer and faster, desperate for more action than he's getting. He wants to get off so bad, but he's fighting it.

Slapping Peyton's ass, I reach beside me in the pocket of my jeans and pull out a condom. I rip it open with my teeth before rolling it over my dick and adjusting it over my piercings. "You ready for me to fuck you hard?" Peyton nods. "You want to see Nico get off on us? I'll make sure you both come; show him how good your pussy is."

"Mmm . . . yes. Please. Just put it in me." She reaches behind her and grips my dick while licking her lips. "It's so big. Will the piercings hurt?"

I lean my head back and moan as she works the head of my dick up and down her folds. Reflexively, she is backing her ass up closer to me. "Fuck me. It won't be the piercings that hurt. Trust me. That's the last thing you should worry about."

Pushing her head down, she frees me from her hold and places both hands flat on the floor. I position my dick at her entrance before shoving it in with one swift movement, slamming against her with force. Her hands grip the carpet as she screams out in pleasure. I still for a second, letting her adjust to my size before pulling it out and ramming back into her a second time. With each hit against her wall, she inches forward slightly, screaming out in a pleasure filled pain. I pick up my speed while yanking back on her hair to keep her still.

"Stroke your cock faster," I demand. "Get yourself off for her."

Nico looks at me with hard eyes. He spits in his open hand and closes it around his dick to give it the effect of her wet pussy, and continues stroking it hard and fast. "Fuck. Her. Harder." He starts moaning and thrusting his hips up and down, fucking his hand. "Shit. This has me so damn hard," he moans.

Smirking, I grab a breast in each hand for leverage to make each thrust harder and deeper. I bend forward and grind my cock each time it disappears inside her completely. Slowly pulling back, I ram it hard at the same time I bite her shoulder. She screams out and a throaty groan sounds out from Nico. "You want a fucking taste? Huh?" I look over at him while slowing my movement down. "Take your jeans off and get down here on your knees."

Nico lets out a long puff before nodding his head and squeezing his eyes shut. "Hell yes." He stands and drops his jeans down to the ground before stepping out of them and yanking his shirt over his head. He's in good shape, but not even close to my build. Still, he's a damn good catch for the ladies.

I pull out of Peyton, but continue to fuck her with my finger, one finger at first, and then two. She's so wet it's oozing out of her pussy. She's still enjoying it. I pull my hand free from her body. "Lay on your back, baby, and spread your legs wide for us."

Peyton does as she's told, baring her clean shaven pussy to us. Nico is now on his knees next to me, eyeing her wet, glistening body as if he's never seen her this way before.

"Good. Now I want you to watch this, Peyton. You want to see how bad he wants you?" She nods her head and looks over at Nico, who is watching her with want in his eyes. "That's my girl." I stand up and grip the back of Nico's head, which gets an instant reaction from Peyton. I like reaction. It's what gets me off. "Does it make you hot to see two men together?"

She lets out something between a moan and a growl, letting us both know what she wants.

Nico runs his tongue over his lips while watching her squirm. His eyes land on Peyton as she reaches down to pull my hand over to her pussy, running it through her folds. He watches the both of us play with her, until finally, he leans in and presses his lips against mine, tasting her sweetness on my tongue. I can feel his body reacting to mine. His body wants what it wants. No judgment here. To me, a kiss is just a kiss. I can partake in the activity without associating it with the gender of who is on the other side. Like I said, it's reaction that gets me off.

Gripping his hair with one hand, I suck his tongue into my mouth before releasing it and pulling away. He's breathing heavily while looking down at my finger buried inside of Peyton. "You like that, Peyton? Huh? You want to see more?"

She nods her head and grabs a breast in each hand, pinching her hardened nipples. She looks him in the eyes, moaning, as she lowers one hand to her clit and begins to rub it as she speaks. "Suck his dick for me, baby." She runs her tongue over her lips. "Do this for me and I'll do anything you ever ask. I promise."

Nico's nostrils flare as he looks down and takes in my size. This is a line we have never crossed, but fuck it. The way I'm feeling at the moment, I could care less whose mouth is around my dick. If it gets her off, then it gets me off.

He hesitates for a moment, looking between the two of us, before leaning down and taking my cock in his mouth. He's gentle at first, clearly uncomfortable, and barely moving until he starts to get the hang of it.

I push my cock further into his mouth as I look down to see Peyton finger fucking herself while she watches him suck my dick. It's evident that she is turned on by this just as much as he is. Her pace increases in speed to match his the faster that Nico takes me.

"She tastes good doesn't she?" I push my dick in further and pull on his hair, causing him to choke a little. "Suck it harder, Nico. You have to get her off by sucking my dick. I don't want to come. I want her to come. Make her come."

He stops for a second to moan before taking it out on me. He takes my dick so hard and fast that it's almost better than most girls I've had. I'm fucking impressed. "You see how much he wants you, Peyton? You see what he's willing to do to get you off? Rub yourself faster, fuck yourself harder, picturing your fingers being his dick." My filthy words coaching her, has her screaming and moaning from another orgasm.

I pull out of Nico's mouth and start stroking my cock. Peyton is crossing her legs from the aftermath of her self-induced orgasm, still playing with her breasts and licking her lips for more. "Get down on all fours. I want you to take my cock in your mouth this time." Hers eyes meet mine as she gets positioned in front of me. She plays with my cock piercings before taking it deep into her mouth and reaching down to play with her pussy. "Get behind her, Nico. Show her how turned on this shit has you."

Gipping her by the hips, Nico gets behind her and slips inside her. He lets out a little moan as he squeezes her ass and slowly starts moving in and out. "Oh shit! Yeah, baby. Suck his dick faster. Take it deep."

I wrap Peyton's hair around my fist and start thrusting my hips faster as her speed picks up. "Fuck yeah, baby. Take it at the back of your throat. I'm about to blow." I feel my orgasm building, so I pull out of Peyton's mouth, yank my condom off, and aim for her mouth.

She opens wide, taking my cock into her mouth, and swallowing every last drop like a pro. I reach over and grab the back of Nico's head, causing him to speed up. The sight of me busting my load in Peyton's mouth pushes him over the edge, and within seconds he is shaking in his own orgasm.

He pushes himself deep, burying his cum as deep as he can. "Holy shit! What the fuck! That feels so damn good." He stills for a second and pulls out before pulling Peyton's body up so that her back is pressed against his chest. He lays one arm across her breasts, cupping the farthest one and runs the opposite hand down her stomach until it's cupping her mound.

She leans her head back and I grab the back of Nico's head, pushing his mouth against hers. He almost pulls back from the taste of me in her mouth, but I reach out and grab his hand, pushing his finger into her wet pussy. She begins grinding her bare ass against him, causing him to go stiff instantly. This is enough to get him going again.

He kisses her harder and deeper while moaning, ready for another round. He watches as Peyton breaks the kiss, lies on her back, and spreads her legs wide before him. I grab his shaft and begin stroking as he watches her. "You see your cum running out of her pussy, Nico?" I increase speed, making him hard as a rock. He nods. "She can hold more . . ."

After a few more strokes, I rub Nico's cock over Peyton's wet little pussy, aligning it with the opening, causing them both to moan out. "Fill her, fuck her, and don't stop until she's filled to max capacity with your cum."

I back away from the two of them as he follows my command. I reach for a damn cigarette and enjoy the show before me. I deserve one after this shit. I should feel some kind of pride for getting them both off and for knowing that they both came here looking for it. But I still feel empty.

There's my screwed up and twisted. This is the person I've become, the life I live . . .

CHAPTER TWO

Hemy

I'M STANDING IN CALE'S KITCHEN waiting on the idiot to gather his shit when Slade walks in wearing his damn suit. I'm never going to get used to this sight. I'm used to him taking clothes off not putting them on. The sleeves to his white button down are rolled up to the elbows, exposing his tattoos, and even I have to admit he looks sort of badass. It makes me want to buy some suits just to strip out of them. That would be a for sure way to pull pussy, not that I have a problem in that area, but it seems women have some sort of fantasy for men in suits. I may just raid his closet later for a trial run.

"Dude." I grip his shoulder and shake him as he reaches in the fridge to pull out a beer. "Since when the hell do you drink beer?"

He smirks while leaning against the fridge and unbuttoning his shirt with one hand. "I told you, man. I'm done with that hard shit. I don't need it anymore."

He takes a swig of his beer. "I can't be all shitfaced when I have a woman to please and a job to do. I'm not fucking shit up."

Wish I would have been that smart.

"Good shit. Where is that sexy little mama anyways? I'm sure she's missing me by now." I wink and grab his beer out of his hand. I get ready to take a drink, but he swats my dick, causing me to groan out as he steals his beer back.

"My bad, mother fucker," he says with a grin. "And hell no. She doesn't miss you. Trust me. I keep my woman well above satisfied. Why do you think we never leave the bedroom?" He gives me a cocky grin.

"It would be better if I joined. You can't deny it," I tease, causing him to tense up. "She's already touched my-"

"Umm. What are you boys doing in here?"

We both look over to see Aspen leaning against the door wearing one of Slade's t-shirts. She smiles at me before turning her attention to Slade and practically growling.

Slade tilts back his beer before shoving it into my chest and walking over to stand in front of Aspen. He presses his body against hers and kisses her neck before picking her up and wrapping her legs around his waist.

"Mmm . . . damn baby. You've been here waiting for me?" Aspen nods her head while biting her bottom lip. "I've been thinking about your sexy ass all day. I need a taste of my woman."

She pulls Slade's bottom lip into her mouth, causing him to growl. "I want to see you strip out of that sexy suit, baby. You know, I still can't get used to seeing you in it, but it's *so, so, so* sexy." I watch as she trails her tongue along his jaw up to the lobe of his ear.

"Oh yeah. Keep on talking like that and I'll take you right here."

Pushing down on my erection, I lean against the counter and eye them both up. "Hell yes. Just don't get mad if I jerk off to you guys fucking. I'll do my best not to join." I pause as they both look over at me. "Unless you want me to. I don't mind getting you both off. My cock is irresistible, so don't complain if you get addicted."

"Fuck off, Hemy." Slade calls over his shoulder as he starts walking away with Aspen. "Save your dick for the private party tonight. I'm sure you'll be using it a lot."

Aspen smiles at me from over Slade's shoulder and I bite my bottom lip as I point at my cock in question. She laughs and shakes her head as I tilt back the bottle of beer.

Aspen and I have a little playful side, but Slade has gotten used to it. He knows I would never really fuck with his woman. Back before, I thought nothing of it, because Slade treated women just as I do now. Nothing but a good fuck to pass the time and get my head off of shit. Things are different now. Slade is a changed man. He's been seeing Aspen for a month now. I've never seen him so damn happy in my life. He even started taking on some cases against drunk drivers or some shit and has completely stopped stripping. He's working hard toward a happy life for them. Aspen is his Onyx. At least he's smart enough to keep her.

Cale passes the happy couple in question and pops into the kitchen. "I'm ready, man. I wanted to wear a uniform or some shit to make it more exciting tonight, but I don't have shit in my closet." Cale runs his hand through his hair while in thought. "I'm tired of just stripping out of my jeans and t-shirt. It's getting boring. Same shit different day."

"Is that right?" I think for a second while finishing off the last of the beer in my hand, before tossing the empty bottle in the trash. "Follow me. I'm sure Slade won't mind if we borrow a couple of his suits. I bet we'll look like fucking studs. If there was a way to wear an invisible sign that said guaranteed mind-blowing orgasm here, this would be it." We rush up the steps to Slade's room.

When I get to his door I hear something fall over and crash to the floor. This fucker really doesn't waste any time. I knock once on the door before pushing the door open and stepping inside.

Oh damn . . .

Slade has Aspen leaned over his dresser with her hands gripping onto the sides. Her upper half is completely bare and pressed against the wood. He has each of his hands locked onto her hips, lifting her feet off the floor, and pounding into her from behind. He notices me walk in through the reflection in the mirror, so he pounds into her one last time and then stops to yell at us.

"Seriously, fuckers? Go ahead, just come on in and enjoy the show! Have some damn respect for Aspen at least. Shit."

I raise my brows at the both of them and walk over to Slade's closet. "I'm offended," I say placing my palm over my heart. "You know damn good and well that I respect your woman. She is one fine piece of ass and she knows it," I tease and wink at her, now staring back at me in the mirror.

She smiles back at my grin, knowing it just revs his engine up more. I knew the girl had a little kinky side buried beneath that shy exterior. I'd be willing to bet she'd let me watch if he would. "Carry on as if we're not even here. Give us a few minutes and we'll be gone. We need to borrow a couple of suits for tonight." I peek over my shoulder and take in the sight of Slade moving in closer to her, as if he's trying to hide what isn't even visible. "Don't keep your lady waiting, Slade." Giving him hell is so much fun, because he's so protective of her.

"You're a real pain in the ass sometimes. You know that?" Aspen growls out trying to feign anger, but I hear the laughter in her tone she is trying to keep hidden. She has to have a sense of humor to deal with me, because I just don't give a shit. "At least Cale is decent enough to peek in from the hallway. Yeah, I see you out there."

Slade lets out a frustrated growl before standing Aspen up from the dresser and covering her nipples with the length of his arm as well as cupping her mound with the opposite hand. He walks them over together to grab Aspen a sheet to cover up with. "Just pick out your damn suits and get the hell out of here. Take them all. I don't care. Just hurry the hell up. I'm putting a lock on my door tomorrow."

Cale steps into the room and laughs. "The dresser? Really?" Slade is wrapping the sheet around her and pulls out when she is covered enough we can't see her.

Slade lights up a cigarette and leans against the dresser with his cock bared for all to see. "Just because I wear a damn suit now doesn't mean shit. What's the fun in sex if you aren't breaking shit and putting holes in the wall? Just hurry up."

"Seriously, dumbass," I jump in. "You would know that if you would actually put your dick in someone. It's fun. Give it a try sometime."

"I plan to, dick. Now let's get these damn suits and go before we're late." Cale shoves me into the closet and reaches for the first suit. "And women don't seem to complain when I use my tongue." He sticks his tongue out and starts waving it around.

"Gross," Aspen calls out. "I don't want to hear that, Cale."

I reach for a slick black suit and toss it over my shoulder. "Alright, man. Let's get the hell out of here.

WE ARRIVE AT THE PARTY and I kill the engine while pumping myself up. It's not very often that we do parties outside of the club, but one of the girls is turning twenty-one and wanted a big blow out. To be honest, I would rather do a house party anyways. More freedom to please the women.

I see the headlights to Stone's Jeep pull up behind us and he quickly jumps out dressed all fly in his own suit. I tug on the sleeve of the white button down before reaching for the black jacket and pulling it on. It's a little tight, but I still look damn good. Cale is wearing a black suit too except his button down is more of a silver color or some shit, maybe gray, hell I don't know. It's cool though. He still looks good.

"You boys better be on your shit tonight," I say while stepping out of my truck. "Especially you, rookie." I point to Stone and shove his shoulder. "Nice fucking suit, man."

He pulls down the front of his suit as if he's all fancy and smirks. "I know." He starts grinding his hips while messing with his buttons. "Once I start grinding, this suit won't even matter." He puts one leg up against his Jeep and starts swaying his hips in a slow motion. "Oh yeah. I'm working my shit tonight."

"Take it easy, lady killer," Cale says with a smirk. "Look." He nods his head toward the small white house and lifts an eyebrow. "The ladies are spying on us."

I tilt my head to the side to take a look. At least six girls are shoved up to the window, watching us with open mouths while fanning themselves off. They're going to need a lot more than a hand to cool them off once we get inside.

I walk over to the door with Cale and Stone trailing closely at my heels. I don't even bother to knock. I just push the door open and step inside. A fast rhythm is playing over the speakers, so I start grinding my body to the music while pulling my tie off and wrapping it around the birthday girl.

She lets out a nervous laugh while checking me out and fixing her tiara. "Oh my . . . yes." She takes a step back and I take a step forward, still grinding my hips. "Best birthday gift ever," she exclaims in a slight slur.

I wrap my hand around to grab the back of her neck before grinding my body against the front of hers and placing her hands on my chest. I don't really pay much attention to the other two, but I assume they are doing something similar from all the screaming that is piercing my ears right now.

Backing the girl up, I walk over to the stereo and change the song. A slow, seductive song comes over the speaker causing my rhythm to become slow and hypnotic. The girl's hands roam my body as I thrust my hips back and forth, close enough for my cock to hit against her stomach. I'm not wearing any briefs, allowing it to hang free. She feels it hardened against her and starts screaming in excitement.

"Oh my god!" She covers her mouth to hide her excitement as I push her against a wall and wrap one of her legs around my waist. "Is this really happening?" She squeals. "This is the best birthday ever. Thank you!"

One of the girls responds from behind me. "Anytime, Jade. Just relax and enjoy. This night is yours."

Her voice sounds a bit familiar, but in the heat of the moment I don't even bother trying to put it together. With both hands I rip my shirt open and watch the girl's eyes widen as she takes in my sculpted body thrusting in her face.

I can feel her wetness on my stomach, because she is wearing a short dress with only her panties between us, so I turn us around until she is sitting on top of a table. I run my hand across it to knock a few things out of the way before pulling my shirt and jacket completely off and throwing it aside.

I hear a few girls scream, so I look over to see Stone already down to a pair of white briefs. He has some girl in a chair and is grinding his dick in her face.

"Holy shit! Take it off! I can feel it on my face," the girl screams. "Oh my God, it's so hard."

"Bite it," another girl screams. "Take me next!" I ignore all the noise behind me and focus on the birthday girl. She's sexy with long red hair and big blue eyes. The dress she is wearing is now pushed up above her hips and she is looking at me as if she's ready to fuck. This drives me wild, especially with everyone watching.

"Just so you know, I'll let the birthday girl touch." I lean into her ear and whisper, "Anything you want."

Her breathing picks up as she looks over my shoulder and then back at me. "I like the sound of that." She smiles and bites her bottom lip. "Dance for me. I've always loved a man in a suit."

I pull her by her thighs so that her body is hanging slightly off the table. I wrap my hands into the back of her hair and press my cock against her heat, while grinding my hips. "Touch me," I whisper. "I'll even let you taste it."

Her hand reaches down in between us as she strokes my cock through the fabric. Her eyes widen as she takes in the size and piercings. "Oh. My. God." She licks her lips and closes her eyes as she strokes it faster. "I'm so damn horny. It's my birthday, you know." She leans in to my neck and kisses it. "No one will mind if I have a little fun. No judging tonight."

"Is that right," I ask. "I can take you right here if you want. I'm here for entertainment and it's what I do best. I'll fuck you here, in front of your friends, and put on a good fucking show."

Reaching down with one hand I undo my pants and pull them slightly down my hips so the tip of my cock is showing. I move my hips into her and start swaying fast as the song picks up in beat. She's leaning into me, moaning, until her eyes land on the tattoo on my side. She eyes it for a few seconds before speaking. "Onyx," she whispers. "Holy shit!" She looks behind me and around for a few seconds before smiling and fingering for someone to come join us. "Look at this. One of the strippers has your name tattooed on him. That is crazy. I don't know anyone else by that name."

I turn beside me to see a woman with platinum blonde curls, tattoos, and piercing green eyes. The whole world crashes around me. It's not just any woman. It's her. It's Onyx. My Onyx. Except . . . she's different now. She's even sexier than I remember and she looks as if she's just seen a fucking ghost. I can't breathe for a moment as I take her in, trying to decide if this is really happening. It's been four years, four fucking years. She is the most beautiful woman, still, to this day.

Her eyes meet mine and her whole body stiffens, but she doesn't speak. Her eyes just take me in as if trying to figure out how I look so different.

Well, damn! I am trying to figure out the same. When did she get all of those damn tattoos and color her hair? She looks wild and dangerous. I love it.

She's stunning, hypnotic, and addicting . . . and I want her.

Four years I have wondered where she's at and here she is right in my damn face.

CHAPTER THREE

Onyx

MY HEART HAS LITERALLY JUST stopped in my chest. *Four years.* I have gone four years avoiding the very man that is standing next to me with his dick practically hanging out of his pants. And of course, it's for another woman. I guess some things never change.

Hemy. My Hemy?

No matter how hard I want to deny it, my traitorous heart gives me away. This man still makes my heart beat wild in my chest and steals my breath away with just one look into those amber eyes. This is going to be hard. Really hard.

It takes every bit of strength in me to pull my eyes away from his gaze. He's looking at me as if he wants to wrap his hands in my hair and pull me into his arms. The pain in his eyes is so intense that it causes an ache in my chest. It's the very look he gave me for the six years we had known each other. What started out as a friendship, turned into something passionate, wild and painful. Very painful. I really tried healing him. I did. But a person can only take so much before they lose control themselves.

I take a step back to compose myself before bringing my eyes down to Hemy's side where sure enough, Onyx is tattooed in big black fancy letters. I feel my throat close up as tears sting my eyes. I won't do this here. I won't show my weakness. I'm different now. I've changed. I'm no longer that weak woman that just let everything slide. I'm much stronger now and no one will break me down again and let me lose myself. Not even . . . him.

"Onyx," Jade squeaks. "Do you see this?" She runs her hand over Hemy's skin causing instant jealousy that I quickly push away. I won't let myself feel. I can't.

I bring my eyes up to meet hers and put on my mask; my game face. "Yup. That is definitely my name. How strange is that?"

Hemy has finally come out of his frozen state and is now staring at me, looking me up and down. I look different. A lot different. But . . . I'm not the only one.

Holy hell!

He runs his hands through his long hair and takes a step away from Jade. His hair is much longer than I remember. It's sexier, making me want to run my hands through it myself. "Onyx," he says in a painful whisper. "What the fuck?" He goes to reach for my chin, but I move away too fast for him to even make contact. "You're back and you couldn't even tell me."

I watch as he rubs his hands over his face in frustration. Of course I didn't tell him. He ruined me. Paralyzed my heart and soul. I wanted to live with him but the truth was, I was doing anything but. I was far from living. I was surviving and he was barely even doing that.

"I'm not doing this, Hemy." I turn to walk away but he grabs my arm to stop me. My heart skips a beat from his touch. "Let go," I snap. "I don't owe you anything. I told you I was leaving and I did. I had to. This is not the time or place." I give him a quick once over, taking in his thick build, tattoos and piercings before yanking my arm from his reach and turning away. "Just do what you're getting paid to do."

Why the hell does he have to look so damn delicious? Even better than before. Not good. Not good at all.

"I'm sorry, Onyx. I had no idea." Jade jumps down from the table and fixes her tiara. "I'll grab another one of the guys. It's not a big deal. You two umm . . . I'm going."

I grab her arm right before she walks away. "No. You won't. *He* is getting paid good money for tonight and he better damn well deliver. I'll be upstairs if you need me."

"Onyx, wait!"

I hold my hand out in front of me and start backing away. "Don't! Just please let my girls enjoy the night. That is all I ask. What we had was in the past. It doesn't matter now." I bite my tongue and walk away as fast as my heels will allow me. I can't let him talk. I can't let myself fall back into him.

I take the stairs two at a time and rush into the bathroom without looking back. As soon as the door closes, my back is pressed against it and I'm falling to the ground with the door supporting me. My hands grip my necklace as I fight to catch my breath. The necklace that Hemy gave me eight years ago. The only piece of him I took with me.

I'm not ready for this yet. I thought it would be different seeing him again. I thought I would be over us. I'm not. I'm so far from it. The truth is, if I hadn't run away when I did, then I would be wrapped up in his arms, clutching him instead of this damn necklace. I came back too soon.

Why do I do this to myself? Why am I still doing it?

Four years of not seeing his face or hearing his soothing voice has been damn near torture. Not a day went by that I didn't wonder where he was or what he was doing. The other problem was, I had to wonder who he was doing. I couldn't allow that to bring me down so I found other things to occupy my time. I can almost see why he did what he did. Almost.

After a few minutes, I calm down enough to push myself back up to my feet. I need to just suck it up. I can't let him see the effect he still has on me. That will only allow him to hurt me again. I won't let that happen.

"Okay. You can do this," I whisper. "He's part of the past. He's part of the past." I try to convince myself but I suck at it. "Dammit."

I stand up tall and take a deep breath before exhaling and pulling the bathroom door open. What I see in front of me causes my breath to be taken away . . . again.

Hemy is standing there still shirtless, just staring at the door as if he had been waiting for it to open.

"Onyx," Hemy whispers. His eyes are soft and caring as they meet mine. Something in them looks different but I can't tell what that means just yet. It's like he's looking at me with different eyes than before. It makes me want to believe he's clean but I know that's almost impossible. "We need to talk about us."

"Hemy," I breathe in frustration. I run my hands through my hair and close my eyes. "There is nothing to talk about. There hasn't been an *us* in a very long time."

I try to step around Hemy, but he places one arm against the wall, blocking me in. "There is an us. There always has been and you know it." He stops and brings his eyes down to my lips. He licks his own and slides his free hand in the back of my hair. "I've missed you, Onyx. I've tried for the last four years to find you but your family are stubborn assholes. I've ended up at their doorstep once a month for the last four years. They're definitely dedicated. I give them that."

Hemy admitting he tried for years to find me shakes something loose inside me that I thought was long lost, but I must remain strong.

I suck in a breath as his body presses against mine. "Hemy." I place my hand to his firm chest to block him from getting any closer. "Please," I plead. "Don't do this to me. It's only going to get you hurt. I don't want to hurt you. Don't make me do it." My eyes land on his lip ring as he bites it. *Damn! I want to bite it too.*

He takes a step back and untangles his hand from my hair before placing it against the wall so I'm completely blocked in. "You already have. You are right now, dammit. I can't believe you didn't tell me you were back. We were friends before we dated and you decided to throw that away as well. You left! You actually fucking left! "

I try to concentrate on what he's saying but him being so close is making it nearly impossible. I can't think straight. Especially when I have a clear view of my name going down his side. It's not only there, but it's huge. It's definitely there for show.

"When did you get my name on you?" I ask while staring at his naked torso. "Why? Why would you do that?"

He drops his arms and takes a step back. "I got it a year after you left. Why? I got it because I couldn't get over you. And I'm still not."

My mouth opens but I can't speak. If I do then it will put me right where I don't want to be. So instead, I just walk away.

"Onyx." I keep going. "Fuck!"

I hear something crash as I walk down the stairs as calmly as I can and try to ignore the fact that Hemy is still into me. All I have to do is make it through this stupid party and then I'll just pretend I never saw him. Pretend that seeing him doesn't still take the breath straight from my lungs.

"There you are." Ash appears at the bottom of the staircase looking up at me. *Shit. Not good.* She brushes her brown curls behind her ear. "Why did you run off? The party is just starting. These boys are so sexy. You need a dance from Stone."

I reach for Ash's arm and pull her around the corner just as Hemy starts walking down the steps. Today is definitely not the day for all this shit to happen. It's too soon and I can't be sure that Hemy has changed. I need to think of something fast.

I press Ash against the wall and force a smile. "Hey. I'm sorry. I was talking to Roman and he needs you to go into work. I would but I really have to be somewhere." I brush her hair behind her ear and try to calm myself. "Is that okay? Would you mind going in? It's Jade's birthday and I-"

"Onyx," she cuts in. "Of course I will go in. I could use the money anyways. No worries. I'll leave now."

She goes to walk away, but I grab her arm to stop her. "Thank you. I owe you."

She flashes me her perfectly sweet smile. "You've already done enough for me. I'll catch you later at home."

I nod my head and lean against the wall as she walks outside. *How the hell am I going to do this? I don't know if I can.*

Hemy appears around the corner with a frustrated scowl on his face. He looks around for a few seconds before his eyes find me. And when they do, they go soft for just a brief moment. "Don't run away again. I can't do this shit, Onyx."

My eyes rake over his gorgeous, toned body before I pull my eyes away and walk toward the door. "I have to go. Just please go take care of Jade. Tell her I had to run out."

I pull the door open and start heading for my Harley. I pull the ponytail holder from my wrist and wrap my hair in it before straddling my bike.

Of course that stubborn ass can't listen and I feel his presence behind me once again. Hemy walks over with wide eyes as I grip the handle and start the engine. "You drive a motorcycle," he says in disbelief. His eyes take in my ride before it finally dawns on him. "Is that my old Harley? You had it fixed up?"

I toss my helmet on and kick the stand up with my foot. "*I* fixed it."

"Since when do you know how to work on motorcycles?"

I give him a stern look and rev the engine. "I learned from the best." I rev the engine again and force a smile, fighting back my emotions. "Actually, I've learned a lot from the best."

His jaw grinds as he watches me drive away. I don't look back. I just drive, needing to escape.

Crap! Crap! Crap!

CHAPTER FOUR

Hemy

ONYX HASN'T LEFT MY MIND once since last night, not that I tried very hard to forget her. After she rode off on my old motorcycle, all I wanted to do was chase after her. I fought so hard not to jump into my truck and chase her down. I know she needs time. I'm trying to respect that, but it's been four damn years already. How much more time could she possibly need?

I stood outside for a good twenty minutes, just staring out at nowhere, until Cale came outside looking for me. Without a word, I followed him inside and went back to work. Nothing about it felt right. All I could think was that I was doing something wrong. How can I feel that way when we aren't even together? She practically hates me, yet I feel bad for stripping for other women. Now isn't that some shit.

"How's that engine coming along?"

I look up when Mitch snaps me out of my thoughts. He's standing on the right side of me, chewing on a sandwich. He's shirtless and equally as dirty and greasy as I am.

"Good. It's all good." I toss down my dirty rag and grab for my t-shirt. "I'm going to head out so I can shower before work. I'll finish this later."

Mitch looks between me and the red mustang I've been working on since eight this morning. He doesn't look happy. He knows something is up, but it's too soon for me to tell him. I don't feel like getting into it just yet. "What's up with you? You've been at this shit for the last eleven hours and now you're about to head out to *Walk Of Shame*? Don't you think you need a break? If I had known you worked tonight then I would have kicked your ass out of my shop a long time ago."

"It's nothing, man." I throw my shirt on and reach in my pocket for a cigarette. "I just wanted to get this shit done. This Mustang has been in the shop since last week and it's not even ready to go yet. I'm sure the owner is ready for his ride back." I brush the loose strand of hair out of my face that has fallen out from the rubber band before lighting my cigarette. "I'll be back after work to finish it."

"Nah, I don't think so. Not tonight. You can finish it in the morning." Mitch takes the last bite of his sandwich before shutting the hood. "This car is off limits until you come back *after* you've gotten some sleep. I hope whatever is bothering you isn't going to make you want to-"

"It's not. Shit, Mitch." I take a long drag of my cigarette and grind my jaw. "I'm done with that shit. You don't need to worry about it." I grip Mitch's shoulder before giving it a shove and walking backwards. "I'm outta here. I'll see your ass bright and early."

"Alright, man. Sorry. Just looking out for ya." He tosses his dirty rag at me and starts walking over to help some scrawny little dude with glasses. "See ya."

"Yup," I mumble, while blowing out smoke. "See ya."

I ARRIVE AT *WALK OF Shame* early and with three shots of Jack and one shot of Patron in my system. The last thing I need to do is let thoughts of Onyx ruin my damn night. I've been doing this shit for too long to care about what someone else might think. Who gives a shit if I strip for the pleasure of women? Onyx left a long time ago. I shouldn't feel guilty. This is me now.

When I walk in, I instantly spot Sara behind the bar. She smiles, but then gives me an *oh shit* look before reaching for a shot glass. "Jack?" She doesn't even wait for me to answer before filling up the shot glass and sliding it in front of me.

I take it and quickly toss it back with a moan. I slam the empty glass down and look around the bar. "It's slow as shit in here."

She smiles. "Because you just got here." She reaches for a glass and mixes a drink for one of her regulars. "They'll start piling in soon. I had at least ten girls ask me if you were working tonight. I told them you'd be in later ready to shake your damn dick. Damn vultures." She hands her regular his drink and then returns to me. "You look like shit by the way."

"Thanks for noticing," I scowl. I scoot my empty glass in front of her. "One more, Sara. You owe me now."

"Damn you, Hemy. I swear you boys have issues. Cale is the only one that doesn't drink his dick swinging life away." She gives me a curious look and gets ready to speak.

"Just do it, dammit."

She rolls her eyes and pours another shot.

The last thing I need is her prying into my business. This is something I need to deal with on my own.

After I tilt back my fifth shot of Jack for the night, I swallow back my pride, stand up, and look back at Sara. "Give me a bottle of whipped cream." Sara reaches in the fridge, tosses it to me, and I catch it and walk away.

I stand in the doorway of the back room for a few minutes pushing my thoughts away, until a slow seductive song plays over the speakers. Without thinking, my body starts moving to the rhythm of the music.

I run my hands down the front of my body while grinding my hips to the beat. My jeans are sitting low on my waist and my button down shirt is rolled up at the sleeves, halfway undone. The girls take notice and instantly start screaming while waving their money around.

Stopping at the first round table I set the bottle of whipped cream down, grab the closest girl's chair, and spin her around to face me. Her eyes go wide as I straddle her lap and grab the whipped cream off the table.

I start grinding my hips to the music, pushing my erection into her as I grab her hands and place them on my chest. "Undo my shirt. Slowly."

She starts doing as told. I tilt my head back and spray whipped cream into my mouth. Reaching beside me, I grab for the sexy brunette close by and run my whipped cream covered tongue across her soft lips, slowly and teasingly. I love teasing these women. It's the perfect distraction.

When I pull away I see the brunette run her tongue over her mouth, licking off every last drop of cream. She sits back in her chair and watches me with hooded eyes, no doubt wanting to taste more.

Noticing that my shirt is now undone and hanging completely open, I yank my shirt off and wrap one of my hands in the back of the blondes hair with one hand, while squirting whipped cream all the way down my chest, stopping at the top of my jeans.

I grind my hips against her one more time before standing up and reaching for the brunette's hand, pulling her to her feet. "On your knees," I command.

She gets down on her knees and all the women start screaming random things.

"Take it off, Hemy!"

"Grab his dick, Katy."

I block out the noise and smirk down at her. "Take my pants off."

Looking up into my eyes, she reaches for my jeans and slowly starts undoing them.

"Faster," someone screams.

That must motivate her, because she yanks my zipper down and rips my jeans down the top of my muscular thighs. I place my hand on her head and push it against the thin fabric of my white briefs.

After rolling my hips a few times, I pull away from her and smear a huge amount of whipped cream down the length of my hard cock. "You ready to get dirty?"

She nods her head as I rub my finger over the fullness of her lips, getting a feel for what's going to be wrapped around my cock. "Lick it off. All of it, from the dirtiest place first."

Running her tongue over her lips, she grabs my waist and leans in to press her tongue against my pelvis, rolling it in the trail of whipped cream. Her eyes watch mine as she slowly lowers her mouth, running her tongue down my defined abs and over my cock.

I wrap my hands in her hair and close my eyes as I slowly rock my hips into her face. I feel her teeth softly nibble my piercings and I yank her head back before stroking my hand over my cock and stepping away from her.

Ignoring the screaming women, I make my way over to the couch, and grab for the chick in a small black dress and heels that is standing up waving money at me.

Gripping her ass, I wrap her legs around my waist and start grinding my hips to the music. I move, slow and deep as if fucking her. She arches her back and wraps her hands in her own hair before sticking a wad of cash in the front of my briefs and moaning out.

I pull her back up and thrust into her one more time before setting her back down to her feet.

Just as I'm about to head over to the next table, I catch a glimpse of a woman with platinum blonde hair and tattoos. I stop dead in my tracks, my heart racing as I watch her, until she turns around to face me.

As soon as I realize it's not Onyx, my heart rate slows down and I let out a breath of frustration. A part of me wishes it were her.

"Fuck!"

I run my hands through my hair and just stand there. The screaming doesn't die down as they wait for me to continue my rounds.

A part of me doesn't want to. I knew this shit would happen. I told myself I wouldn't let myself think about her anymore. Yeah, well great fucking job.

"Hemy. Dude!"

I snap out of it enough to see Stone approaching. He grips my shoulder and pushes my chest. "What the hell is up, man? You're just standing here. You've been acting funny since last night."

I push his hand away and grind my jaw. "Nothing. I just needed a second." I pause and exhale, hating myself for what I'm about to do. "I have to go."

"What the hell? What do you mean?"

I grab for my jeans and start heading for the door. "I have somewhere I have to go. It's important. I need you to take over my room."

Stone gives me a confused look, but doesn't question me further. "Sure. Yeah. Go then."

I walk through the bar, past Sara who gives me a confused look, and outside over to my truck. I quickly hop inside and shove my keys into the ignition while tossing my jeans into the passenger seat. As stupid as I know I'm being, I know it's smarter than just letting her walk away again. I refuse to let her disappear from my life now that I've found her. There's always been something about her that draws me in, holding me to her. It's a curse as much as a craving.

I start the engine and pull out onto the dark street. Without a second thought, I head toward the house I saw her at last night. I don't give a shit what anyone thinks. I'm going to find out where she's at and I'm going to make her mine. Her and I both know that we are meant to be together. The hard part is making her see that, making her see the new me.

After about ten minutes, I find myself pulling up in front of the small white house. I kill the engine, grab for my jeans, and hop out to put them on.

Just as I'm buttoning them, the front door opens and two girls walk out. I notice one of them right away: Jade.

She gives me a curious look before smiling and walking over to me.

"Look who's back," she says teasingly. "You come back for your tie?"

I lean against my truck and look over her shoulder at the door. "It's not what I forgot, it's who," I say firmly. "Where can I find Onyx?"

Jade quickly turns away and starts heading for the little black car that is sitting in the driveway. "I don't know," she calls over her shoulder. "I'll let her know you're looking for her."

I quickly catch up to her and grab her arm. "Tell me." I walk over to stand in front of her. I look into her eyes so she knows how important this is to me. "I need to know where she is. Can you just tell me where to find her?"

She lets out a breath of frustration before looking over at the other girl who nods at her. She turns back to me and rolls her eyes. "Follow us. She's at work and we're heading there now. I'm going to get in deep shit for this," she mumbles.

"Thank you, Jade." I don't waste any time jogging over to my truck and jumping inside. I've waited too damn long for this shit and she's going to listen to what I have to say.

I follow the little black car for what seems like forever. In reality it was probably a whole fifteen minutes. Still, fifteen minutes too long, and now I'm anxious as shit.

When we pull up in front of the huge black building, I sit there wondering if this is some kind of joke. There's no way that the Onyx I knew would work at a place like this.

I sit here for a few minutes until I see Jade and the other girl get out of the car. Jade looks over at me and waves her arm for me to follow. "You coming or what?"

I take a deep breath to calm myself before getting out of my truck and slamming the door behind me. Every part of me wants to scream and break something. The idea of her working here makes me sick to my stomach. "Vixens Club," I growl to myself while staring up at the neon sign.

She's a damn Vixen? A stripper . . . like me. Well fuck me.

CHAPTER FIVE

Onyx

"OKAY, GIRLS, JUST REMEMBER TO have fun. This is free night. You are welcome to roam as you wish. Just remember the rule: no touching unless you put their hands there. You know what to do if someone breaks the rule. I'm sure there's no need for me to go over it again."

I get a few head nods from the girls and a hell yeah from Ash.

I stand up from straddling my chair and walk in front of it, facing my group of girls. The first shift of the night is almost done, and I made sure that all of my girls work together all night. I always stress their safety on free nights. I don't like the idea of not being able to keep my eye on them individually. There are quite a few creeps that come in here and I would hate to have to break a heel off in a few of their asses. That's why I have "the talk" with my girls once a week.

"Alright, ladies. Let's get ready to make some cash then." I smile and head over to my makeup station as the other girls head over to the floor.

I've been hiding in the back for the last twenty minutes. I'm not really sure why, but my game seems to be a bit off tonight. I keep telling myself it has nothing to do with Hemy. The truth is, I'm not very convinced. I could never convince myself of anything when it came to him. I went to sleep with him on my mind and woke up with him on my mind. I guess not much has changed over the years.

"Shit. Stop thinking, Onyx." I rub my hands over my face and take a deep breath. "He'll only hurt you again. Don't do this to yourself. You finally got rid of that pathetic little girl that was nothing but a doormat for him."

I curse to myself when I feel a hand grip my shoulder. I have no idea who it is or how much of my rambling they have heard, but I suddenly feel really nervous. I'm not ready to explain Hemy to anyone. I'm not sure I'll ever be.

"What's going on, Onyx?" Jade takes a seat at the makeup table next to mine and starts digging through her makeup bag. "Something's been bothering you since last night. You can talk to me . . ."

"I'm fine." I force a smile and look at myself in the mirror. My blonde curls are wild tonight and my makeup is a little too dark on the eyes. I look a lot different than I did four years ago. I can't even imagine what Hemy must have thought when he saw me at the party last night. He seemed a little shocked, but couldn't seem to keep his eyes off of me. It made my heart race, making it hard for me to think straight.

I let out a little laugh and stand up, fixing my black lingerie. It's barely covering anything, yet it makes me feel more confident and alive than I have felt in years. "You know I just get a little stressed on free nights. I worry about you girls roaming around where I can't see you all. That's all."

Jade gives me a look as if she wants to say something. She almost looks nervous. She opens her mouth a few times and then shakes it off before starting in on her makeup. "Yeah. I know," she says softly. "We do fine though. You taught us all well. Stop worrying so much."

I stand here for a few seconds before I realize that Lily isn't here yet, or that I've seen. The girls usually show up together since they're roommates. "Where's Lily?"

Jade nervously clears her throat while walking over to the closet to grab her outfit. "She's here. She'll be back in a minute. She's, ah . . . showing someone around."

"Alright," I say softly. She's definitely acting a bit strange right now and I'm not so sure that I like it. "I'll see you out there."

"Sounds good. See you in a few."

After walking through the door, it takes my eyes a couple minutes to adjust to the dim lighting. The music is playing loud and the room is filled with a light fog so I can barely make out Ash and the other girls dancing at tables for the overly eager dirtballs.

I barely get ten feet into the room before I am called over to a table. Although I'm still feeling a bit off, I shake it off and walk over with a seductive smile.

"Hey, boys," I say sweetly.

"Mmm . . . very nice." One of the three men holds up a handful of cash as I lean over and grab his tie, winding it up in my hand. I hear him let out a little moan, so I wrap it tighter and pull myself to him, straddling his chair.

"So you like it rough, big boy?" I yank his hair back and starting moving my hips to the music, grinding myself against his erection.

He bites his bottom lip and gets ready to place his hand on my ass, but I yank his hair as hard as I can, causing him to growl. "Damn, you're rough, baby," he says with a hint of laughter. "I would love to see the things you do in bed."

"That won't be happening," a deep, rough voice growls behind me.

My heart instantly drops to my stomach as soon as the words leave his lips. It doesn't take me having to look behind me to know who it is. I've heard that voice a million times before and I'll never forget it. The only difference is, now it has a deeper edge to it.

"Excuse me," the guy below me bites out. He lets out a sarcastic laugh and places a possessive arm around my waist. "She's in my lap. Wait your turn. *If* it ever comes."

With my left hand, I choke him with his tie while yanking his head back with my right. "Don't ever touch me again."

The guy starts choking and I look back at Hemy to see his fists balled at his sides. I don't need him to protect me. He has a history of fighting and that's the last thing that I need him doing right now. He would kill this guy. This douchebag is nowhere even close to Hemy's huge build.

"Don't even think about it, Hemy." I push away from the guy and he starts fighting for air and pulling at his tie. "What the hell are you doing here?"

"Crazy, bitch," the guy chokes out through breaths.

Hemy looks down at the guy with a hard look, so I place my hand across his chest and push him away.

He takes in a deep breath and exhales, his jaw steeled. I can tell he's fighting really hard right now to keep his control. "I could ask you the same," he growls. "This place isn't you."

"Ha!" I walk away from him, but he keeps following at my heels. "Like you have room to talk. You're a male stripper. Do I need to remind you of that?"

He grabs my arm to stop me from walking. "Yeah, and I'm a piece of shit. That is the difference." He turns me around to face him and backs me up against the wall with his arms and body blocking me in. "You are too good for a place like this. What the hell, Onyx? You could get hurt here. I would fucking kill someone for hurting you. Do you get that?"

I find an empty room in the back and push him into it. Then I turn away and fight to calm my breathing.

Neither of us speak for a few minutes.

"What are you doing here, Hemy? How did you . . ." I stop as I put the pieces together. "Damn you, Jade," I whisper.

I feel the warmth of Hemy's body as he steps up behind me. A part of me wants to lean into him, but the rational part of me moves away. "I can't stop thinking about you, Onyx. You've been on my mind every day for ten years." He wraps an arm around my waist and presses his body against mine. It feels good. So damn good. "Don't tell me I haven't been on yours," he whispers, leaning into my ear. "Tell me I've been on your mind." He pushes my hair behind my ear before brushing his lip piercing up my neck. "Say it."

I let out an unwanted moan as my eyes close to his touch. The feel is so familiar, yet it feels so much better than before. My body is reacting in a way it hasn't reacted to anyone but him. It's unstoppable. "Yes," I admit while finally pulling away and spinning around. "You have. What do you expect? You hurt me. You broke my heart, dammit."

He lets out a frustrated groan and runs a hand through his short beard. *That sexy beard.* I can't help but to imagine it rubbing against my naked flesh. Everything about Hemy is sexier than I remember. He's taller, thicker, full of tattoos and has long, thick, hair that I want to pull. Not to mention those piercings. It makes me wonder where else he might be pierced. He always was the wild one.

"I'm not the same person I was back then." My eyes land on his bare chest as he takes a step toward me. "I'm different now."

"Oh yeah?" I swallow as I reach out to trace his tattoo with my fingers before pulling away. "How so?"

He wraps his hands into the back of my hair and presses me against the wall with his body flush against mine. "I would give my last breath to be with you." He looks into my eyes with an intensity that makes my knees go weak. "I will stop at nothing to make you mine, Onyx. I'm not letting you run away from me again, from us. You can hurt me all you want. You could stomp on me till I'm no longer breathing and it wouldn't make a difference. I'm. Not. Going. Anywhere."

Inside, I am going crazy. I can't think straight and my body feels like giving out on me. I can't give myself away though. As much as I wish I could, Hemy can never be trusted.

"Hemy," I say firmly. "Don't start something you're not going to like. I'm not letting myself get crushed by you again. Things are different now. You're not the only one that has changed. Do you get what you put me through?" I place my hands on his chest and push him away. "How many girls had their hands on you, how many nights I cried myself to sleep not knowing if you were even alive."

"I'll be with you every fucking night. You'll never have to worry about that shit again." He pounds his fist into the wall before placing both hands against it. "I'll wake up next to you and fall asleep holding you for the rest of my fucking life. Nothing else matters anymore. I've learned to let go and move on."

I suck in a burst of air and cover my face. Those are the words I longed to hear for so long in the past and they never came. Hearing those words makes my heart feel as if it's about to burst out of my chest. The ache is so strong that I have to grip my chest.

"Onyx!" Roman pokes his head into the door and looks between me and Hemy. "What are you doing? I've been looking for you." He gives me a concerned look. "Is he giving you problems?"

Hemy turns away from the wall and pops his neck. "Who the fuck are you?"

I hold my hand out and place it on Hemy's chest. "He's my boss," I snap. I turn to face Roman. "No, and he was just leaving."

Roman looks Hemy up and down one last time before turning back to me. "You have a private dance waiting in room six. Don't keep them waiting too long."

I nod my head and give Hemy a dirty look. "Okay. I'm almost done."

Hemy watches with dark eyes as Roman walks away. He looks like he's ready to kill someone. "A private dance?"

I give him a little push toward the door. "Yes. You need to go."

He walks out the door and starts looking around at the room numbers.

"What are you doing," I bite out. "The exit is that way." I point over to the exit sign, but he ignores me and starts heading for room six. "Are you kidding me?" I follow behind him and we both stop in front of the door.

"It's my turn to see you dance." He turns to me and flashes a cocky grin. "You want to dance for me, baby?" He leans in and kisses my neck. "Because I'm not going anywhere."

"No." I lightly tug his hair back, causing him to growl. "The point of a private dance is for it to be private, Hemy. There's no way my client is going to be okay with you joining."

"Oh yeah," he says. "I wouldn't be so sure about that." He yanks the door open and walks inside. His eyes set on the handsome guy with blonde hair wearing a business suit, holding a bottle of beer to his lips. He pulls out three hundred dollar bills and slaps it down in front of him. "I'm paying for the second dance." Then he pulls back a chair and sets it so he's sitting on the side of the client, but facing him. "You have a problem with that?"

The business guy looks at Hemy, a little intimidated and then down at the pile of money in front of him. "No, man. Not at all," he slurs. "Enjoy the show."

Now pissed, I slam the door behind me and yank Hemy's head back by his hair before whispering, "Just remember you did this to yourself." I push his head forward and walk over to the man in the suit.

I grab his beer from out of his hand and toss it across the room. I'm pissed. Not only at Hemy, but at this drunken idiot for agreeing to let him watch. I lift my leg, placing my heel next to him on the couch. I dig it into the leather while grabbing him by the tie and yanking his head to my breasts.

I squat so that I'm closer to his waist. I start to sway my hips to the slow rhythm while running my hands through his hair and rubbing my breasts over his lips.

I allow myself to get lost in the music playing over the speakers, doing this for a few minutes before releasing his tie, and pulling his head back by his hair. I look down at his lap and smirk. "Someone's already hard for me." Opening the top of my black bustier, I straddle his lap and start grinding myself against his erection.

The guy starts moaning while looking down at my breasts and licking his lips. "Oh yeah, baby. Keep rubbing against my dick."

I don't usually talk much with the men in private dances, but having Hemy in the room somehow makes me want to have a little fun. After all those years of me sitting by, while women touched and enjoyed him, why not give him a little taste?

"Mmm . . . you like that, big boy?" I rip his shirt open and grab onto it while arching my back and rolling my front against his. "It's so big and hard for me."

I grind my hips faster while moaning out and biting my bottom lip. I place my hands on my hips and roll with the beat of the music, popping my ass with each one. I trail my hands upward and continue the slow hypnotic motion of the dance. I stop briefly when I reach my breasts that are peeking out of my top. I can feel his eyes on me, both of them. I close my eyes and continue my path upward until I reach my long blonde hair.

The heels of my black leather knee-high boots are pressed into the leather of the sofa. I keep my balance steady as I grind against his cock. My eyes remain closed. I fist through my hair, messing it, as I seduce him with my movements.

I sit up and tease him in reverse, running my hands down my breasts, down my stomach and in between my ass and his hard on, while looking over at Hemy.

His eyes go hard as he reaches down to adjust his cock. Seeing him hard gets me even more excited. It actually has me turned on. Our eyes lock as I grasp Mr. Professional's cock in my hand and start rubbing myself faster while stroking it through the fabric.

The guy starts moaning and gripping onto the couch as his cock starts throbbing in my hand.

I stand up and turn back around with my pussy in his face as he comes in his fancy slacks.

"Oh fuck," he moans while rubbing his hands over his face. "That was fast."

I look at Hemy and smirk. "That was fast."

Hemy runs his hand over his cock, but looks pissed. I can tell he wants to get off too. Hemy's not as easy as this guy was. He needs more. "Now, it's time for round two."

"Are you sure you can handle round two?"

A rumble comes from Hemy's chest. "If I can handle losing you, I can handle anything."

Now my focus is all on wanting Hemy to come for me. As bad as it sounds, I need this. I'm wound so tight right now, and that's all I need to push me over the edge.

I pick up the three hundred dollar bills and hand them to the messy guy that couldn't hold his shit. "Leave," I say. "You should probably go clean up."

My eyes meet Hemy's and they stay there as the man quickly leaves us alone.

"Lock the door," I demand. Hemy follows him and locks the door with a smirk before he walks over to stand in front of me. "No touching," I state. "Just yourself."

Hemy grabs me by the hips and sets me on top of the table before walking away and taking a seat on the other side of the couch. The clean side.

His eyes watch me with heated desire as I open the rest of my bustier and pull it open. My hands reach up to rub my pierced nipples, causing Hemy to growl and adjust his cock.

"Mmm . . . you like that?" I run my hands in between my breasts until they reach the top of my panties. "I want you to come for me, Hemy. I miss seeing you lose it over me."

He watches me as I drop down on my knees and spread my legs apart. I slowly slide my hand down the front of my panties and run my finger up and down my wetness before sliding a finger inside. "Mmm . . . I'm so wet for you." I push in and out. "Can you hear it, Hemy? Remember how much you loved the sound of me being wet for you?"

"Fuck yes." He undoes his jeans before pulling down the zipper. "Fuck yourself faster and rub your nipple with your other hand." I do as he says while moaning out. "That's it, baby. Do it for me."

I position myself so that I'm sitting on my ass with my legs spread eagle in front of his face. I want to be sure he gets a good view. Then, I pull my panties to the side and bare my wet, throbbing, pussy to him.

"That's it, Onyx." He pulls his cock out of his jeans and I instantly notice the piercings. It has me so turned on that I have to stop all movement in fear of getting off too soon. He notices me eyeing his cock and grins. "Imagine these steel bars deep inside you as I pound into you. You know I like it deep, baby." His hand starts stroking his cock and I instantly notice the bead of pre-cum that drips off the head and onto his hand.

I bring my hand down to touch myself again and move at the same rhythm Hemy is, as he strokes himself. His eyes never stray away from my fingers shoving themselves deep inside me.

I've needed this for a long time. Ever since leaving Hemy, reaching orgasm has become almost close to impossible. Just watching him get off as I get myself off is enough to make me want to explode.

He starts stroking harder and faster while sucking on his lip ring. "I'm about to blow, baby. I wish it were inside of you."

His words set me off and I find myself shaking from the most intense orgasm I have had in years. A few seconds later, Hemy is blowing his load into his free hand, moaning out my name.

We both look at each other while coming down from our temporary high.

He reaches for a clean towel and wipes his hand off. "We still need to talk."

I cover myself back up and close my eyes. "I don't have time right now. I'm working."

Right as I'm about to close my legs, his eyes meet the inside of my right thigh.

He jumps out of his chair and grips my thigh to hold it open. "What the fuck is that?" He spreads my legs wide open and runs his hand over my tattoo while breathing heavily. "You got my name tattooed on you?"

I never meant for him to see that. It was for my own private reasons. The lettering is so small that you can barely even make out what it says unless you look extra close. "Not now, Hemy. I'm not getting into this."

He growls as I push his hands away and force my legs closed. "That was my favorite spot. I would kiss you there almost every night before bed. Is that why you did it?"

I'm not answering that. This was a horrible idea but I needed to get off.

"I don't have time for this." I climb off the table and walk toward the door with speed. I get ready to open it, but get stopped by Hemy's voice.

"Come to my work when you have time." He walks past me and stops to look back at me with hurt eyes. "I'll always make time for you. I won't break anymore promises."

I stand there and watch him as he walks away. He knows damn well that he has me hanging on again. The question is . . . how tightly?

Well that went well . . .

CHAPTER SIX

Hemy

IF ONYX THOUGHT FOR ONE minute I was going to back off she really doesn't remember how persistent I was when it came to her. Now that I've gotten another glimpse at what's been mine all along, there is nothing that can stop me from claiming her as mine again. I'm a lot stronger than I was back then. My head is a lot clearer. I know what I can't live without and without a doubt that is her.

Knowing that she has my name permanently inked on her skin is fucking with me so bad that I can't even think straight. She can get my name tattooed on her body, but she acts as if she doesn't want shit to do with me. It has my chest aching at just the thought.

"A fucking tattoo, man," I mumble while looking back up at Cale. "My name branding the inside of her perfect little thigh. Do you know how bad that screws with my head?"

He watches me as I take a long drag of my cigarette and slowly exhale. "I guess you both had it a lot deeper than you thought, man. She obviously loved you and missed you or else she wouldn't have gotten it. Plus, no other guy wants to see that shit, so I doubt she's seriously dated anyone since you. Think back to when you got yours. What made you do it?"

I take another drag while running my hand through my hair. I don't even need to think about this one. "I missed her so damn bad that the thought of her made it hard to breathe. It still does, man. It's been four damn years and I feel exactly the same about her. It kills me to think about all the time we have missed out on. No other girl compares to her, never will. They are simply temporary fill ins for what I wish I still had." I toss my cigarette and pull both hands through my hair in frustration. "I'm getting her back, man. I don't care what it takes."

Cale nods his head in understanding and grips my shoulder. "Make sure she sees that. It may hurt a shit ton getting there, but it will be worth it in the end. All she has to do is see that." He watches me as I toss my cigarette down and rub my hand down my short beard. "It's all good, man. You need to relax a bit. Give it some time. You remember that stupid shit saying we used to hear as adolescents? The one that goes, if you love something set it free and if it comes back it was meant to be?"

I look up; my interest slightly peeked. "Well, she's back isn't she? Time, man. Just give it time."

"Yeah. Sure," I mutter. "Time . . . because four years isn't enough damn time." I walk past Cale and into my garage, shoving my head back under the hood of his truck.

It's been five days since I have seen Onyx and I'm starting to go insane. My patience is wearing thin and I'm not sure how much longer I can wait before I show back up at *Vixens* and take her my damn self. I'm doing my best not to push her away again. It's a lot harder than I expected, so I'm spending my time trying to occupy myself anyway I can.

I'm lost in my own little messed up world, doing my best to concentrate on Cale's truck, when I hear a set of heels pounding up the driveway.

"Holy shit," Cale mumbles. "If you are Onyx then I can see why my guy is so screwed up in the head right now."

I toss down my wrench and grip the edge of the hood, trying my best to keep my cool. The thought of Onyx possibly being here gets my heart pounding. I try my hardest not to get my hopes up, but knowing that she has no clue where I even live is making it slightly difficult. It could be one of numerous girls that I have brought here in the past, but what if it's her? That means she premeditated coming here and had to find out from someone else how to get here.

"So, you've heard of me?" Onyx's voice comes out cool and calm, causing my grip on the hood to tighten. "Hemy."

I release the hood and turn around to face her, leaning my back against the truck. I look her over in her short black shorts and white tank top. I can't help but to admire her stunning beauty. She always did take my breath away, even before the dark side took her, but I can't deny it looks damn sexy on her.

Her legs are long, slender and well sculpted, making those shorts look as if they were made just for her. Perfection. They're hard not to stare at, and her hair that was once a strawberry blonde is now a platinum blonde, her curls falling just below her tight little ass. The sight of her is enough to take any man's breath away.

"I'm guessing you paid Mitch a visit?" She nods her head. "Yeah. Figures he wouldn't tell me."

I tilt my head to Cale before reaching in my pocket for my keys. I toss them to him and he quickly catches them. "What's this for, man?"

"Take my truck. Come back after work and I'll have yours ready." I give him an impatient look as he just stands there staring. "Any day now."

Cale looks at Onyx while backing away with a smirk. "Take it easy on the guy." He winks before turning away and jogging to my truck.

Onyx walks over and stops right in front of me. Her eyes search mine for a moment before she pulls them away. "I need to ask you something and I need you to be-"

"Yeah," I answer, already knowing what her question is going to be. It's the one thing she wanted the whole time we had been together. "I'm clean. For three years now."

She looks back up and her eyes soften for a brief moment before she puts her guard back up. "How do I know you're telling the truth? That kind of life isn't easy to give up."

I take a step closer and lean down close to her face. Our lips are so close to touching that it takes all my strength to not kiss her. "I may have been a piece of shit, but did I ever lie to you?"

Hurt flashes in her eyes before she quickly shakes it off. "I don't know," she whispers. "Do you even know?"

A pain aches in my chest, knowing what she means. I was so damn messed up most of the time that I don't even remember a lot of shit that happened. "I would like to believe that I know." I wrap my hands in the back of her hair liked I used to in the past. Her eyes close as I start to massage my fingers through it. "I've missed this."

I press my body against hers, causing her to let out a small moan. "I can't think when you touch me like this, Hemy. You should stop. Now," she says breathless.

"I can't think when I *look* at you. I never could." I turn us around and back her into the garage and against Cale's truck. I can tell how much my body against hers is breaking her willpower, and I can't help but to use it to my advantage. I press my leg between her thighs and grind into her. "You feel good in my arms, baby. You see how good this feels?"

"Hemy. I didn't come here for this."

"Answer me," I breathe. "We've always been honest with each other. Don't change that now."

She lets out a small breath and tangles her fingers in the back of my hair. "Yes," she moans. "Physically it feels great. Emotionally, it terrifies me. I'm not letting you in, Hemy. I've learned my lesson."

I run my hands down her back before cupping her ass in my hands and running my lips up her neck. "Oh, but I want in. Deep." I suck her earlobe into my mouth before whispering, "You remember what it feels like to have me inside you? The way you moaned out my name and pulled my hair. That mix between pain and intense pleasure. It can be even better now."

Her head tilts back as she falls into my touch. I can hear her breathing pick up as I squeeze her ass tighter. "Don't make me think about sex. It brings back bad memories." She grips onto the hood with one hand as I kiss her neck. "Questions. The fear of you being with other women. All those hands groping you. How am I supposed to get over that? Maybe I want a little fun of my own."

My body stiffens from her words. As much as I hate it, she's right; because of my fuck up she had to live in fear of me being touched by other women. The thought makes me sick now. I need to somehow make it up to her. "What do you need? I'll fucking do anything for you."

"Do you realize how many women I had to see touch you while you were passed out? Every time I close my eyes I picture someone's hand down your pants. Their hands on my man. That image does a lot of damage. You'll never get that until you have to deal with it yourself. I just can't. I can't be with you like that again, Hemy. Ever."

Her grip tightens on my hair as I wrap mine in the back of hers and lean my forehead against hers. "I can arrange that," I grumble. "I'd have to fight my hardest not to kill someone, but I get where you're coming from. I would do it. I would watch it even though the thought kills me."

She looks at me in shock and laughs in disbelief. "Are you joking?" I shake my head and her face becomes serious. "And what if I want a threesome? Would you do it? With another man?"

I brush her hair over her shoulder and kiss her neck, then her chin. "If it involves me touching you or tasting you . . . then yes. I will do anything you tell me to. Even that."

She pushes away from me and turns around. "Shit, Hemy. I was joking." She grips the top of her hair and tilts her head back. "Why did you have to say that? You're supposed to make it easy to not want you in that way. I'm not supposed to want to touch you, but I do. No man turns me on like you can and it drives me mad."

I don't want to hear about other men. I just want her anyway I can. "Stay with me tonight." I know her answer will be no, but I try anyway. "You don't have to let me in emotionally; not yet at least. Just let me take care of your needs."

"Hemy," she warns. "I have to work tonight, and that's a horrible idea. Do you realize what kind of shit that will start?"

"Yes," I admit. "Why do you think I asked?"

"Dammit, Hemy. I have to go." She takes off walking down the driveway as fast as she can on her tall heels. "Bye."

Without a second thought, I jog down the driveway, grab her by the waist, and turn her around to face me. "Not yet. There's something I've been waiting four years to do." I grip the back of her head and slam my lips against hers, running my tongue over the seam of her lips for access.

All of my breath leaves my body as she opens up and kisses me back, her arms snaking around my neck.

It feels like the past four years disappearing between us and it feels like we are back in the past. My tongue desperately seeks hers, sucking it into my mouth as I back her up against a little blue car and cup her face in my hands.

Pressing my body against hers, I tug on her bottom lip before releasing it. Both of us stand here panting while looking into each other's eyes. I can barely catch my breath.

Standing here, looking in her eyes, I realize the distance between us still remains and I have a lot of work to do in order to close the gap. But I'm willing and in it for the long haul.

"I never want to hear bye come out of your mouth again. I'll be waiting for you. I've waited for four years. Don't think I will give up now."

I turn and walk away before she can say anything. I don't want her to. I want her to think about the last thing said between us. It gives me more confidence that she will show up at my doorstep tonight.

I hear a car door slam behind me, but I refuse to turn around. I never want to have to see her driving away from me again.

Within a few seconds, she starts the car and I hear it pull away. I walk over and stand in front of Cale's truck for a few minutes before walking inside and grabbing my phone.

I dial Nico's number and wait for him to answer.

"Yo. What's up, bro?"

I grind my jaw and take a deep breath. "I need you to do me a favor. Tonight.

Damn. I can't believe I'm doing this . . .

I PULL MY HARLEY INTO the back of *Walk Of Shame* and kill the engine. I haven't stopped thinking about my plans for tonight since Onyx drove away from my house. It's had me on edge all damn day.

I'm here to ease my mind a bit. Not to get plastered, but to douse the anger that is building inside at the thought of another man touching Onyx. I want to protect her, but at the same time . . . I want her back. I want to take care of her needs and ease her mind.

It may hurt like a bitch, but I deserve it. I hurt her far worse than I can ever imagine. I was her weakness. I broke down her walls while keeping mine up. I was too broken to let her in. I had lost everyone that I loved in life and I was afraid of letting myself love anyone else. I was afraid that if I lost one more person that it would push me over the edge. The day she walked out my door was the day I realized I had loved her all along. Made me realize I wasn't as damaged as I thought.

This is her payback. I need to feel her hurt, drown in my own pain and suffering. I'll do whatever it takes and you better believe I won't back down.

I see Stone as soon as I walk through the door. He nods to me with a wink while grabbing some chicks head and grinding his cock against her face.

I nod back and go to find Cale at the bar. It's a Tuesday night; it's one of our slowest days.

"What's up, man."

Cale slides a glass in front of the girl across from him before cashing her out and slipping the change into his tip jar.

"Not shit." He smiles, flashing his deep set of dimples. "Just enjoying this relaxing night. I sometimes forget how nice it can be to just bartend. No screaming girls in my damn ear. You know?"

"I hear ya." I pull out my wad of cash and throw him a ten. "Give me a beer."

Cale reaches below him in the fridge and slams a beer down in front of me. "You look like you need one. Things didn't go well with your girl?"

I give him a hard look and grind my jaw, trying to keep my cool. "Depends on what the hell you consider good." I tilt back my beer and look up at him. "Let's just say I arranged a little fun for her tonight and it has me a little on edge." I run my hand through my hair and tilt my head back. "I deserve it though. I have no right to be mad."

"Ouch. You just have to think of it this way. At least she wants you there for her *fun*. She could want to do whatever that is without you. It's a step, my man."

I nod my head while slamming back more of my beer. I sit here in silence for a moment and try my best to think of the positive shit this could lead to. "I suppose your ass is right. If it's one step closer to making her mine again then I'll do it and show her how far I'm willing to go for her this time."

Cale jumps up to sit on the bar and slaps my shoulder. "Right on. You know no woman can resist the Hemy charm."

I tilt my head up and give him a dirty look. "She left me, asshole. It obviously doesn't work on her."

"Yeah. And that's why you have to show her the new Hemy charm. Has any other woman been able to resist you?"

I shake my head while finishing off my beer.

"Exactly!" He jumps down from the bar and fetches me another beer. "She'll come around. Now drink that and get the hell out of here. I have shit to do."

He backs away with a smile while giving me the middle finger with both hands before turning around and helping another customer.

I'm going to please my woman and make her mine again. I don't care how . . .

CHAPTER SEVEN

Onyx

I'VE BEEN OFF WORK FOR the last hour, trying to get my head straight. I spent the whole night lost in thoughts of Hemy, and trying to decide what I should do. He hurt me. He hurt me numerous times and the visions I have of him playing in my head are like a poison. They're draining me bit me bit, making it hard to even function.

We weren't supposed to meet up like this. I was supposed to have more time to prepare. I was hoping he wouldn't recognize me at first and that I would have more time to feel him out, to see if he has changed. I have something to tell him. This is something that will change his life forever, but I need to know that he is clean, and the only way to do so is to spend time with him.

I have no idea how I'm going to be able to hang out with him without wanting him. That's why I have to be careful. I have to do whatever I can to keep him at a distance, and to keep my heart safe. The kiss that he surprised me with still has my heart beating wild and my legs trembling. It was all too familiar and reminded me of what I've been missing.

"You can do this," I whisper while looking into the mirror. "You'll just go there and feel him out." I grip the sink and close my eyes.

I need to do this. The only problem is, I have no idea what he has planned. Hemy is wild. If he thinks I want a threesome with him and another man, he'll find a way to make it happen. He has a way of getting anything that he wants. He's better at this than I am. That's why I have to push back and not give him the alone time he needs to win me back. If he wants me physically, the only way I'll be safe is by making him share me. Once he gets me alone, he wins.

I open my eyes and take a deep breath as the bathroom door pushes open to Ash peeking in. Her dark curls fall over her shoulders when she smiles. "Hey," she whispers.

I force a smile and choke back my emotions. I know I'm doing the right thing. "Hey, sweetie," I reply. "You do good on tips tonight," I ask as a distraction.

She pushes the door open and leans against the frame. "I did great on tips." She looks me over and frowns. I guess the distraction didn't work. "What's been up with you tonight? You've been acting strange. Is everything alright?"

Not really. Not yet. "I'm good," I lie. "I'm just feeling a little off tonight." I push away from the sink and turn to walk toward the door. "There's an old friend of mine that I haven't seen in a while. It's just bringing back a lot of old memories."

She smiles in understanding and nods her head. "Memories are the last thing I want to think about. Hopefully yours are a lot better than mine."

I run my hands over my dress to dry my sweaty hands. If only she knew. "Some are good." I smile. "I'm heading out for a while. I'll be back."

She takes a step back, allowing me to walk through the door. "Onyx." I stop and turn around. "Will I get to meet this old friend?"

I swallow and nod my head. "Someday."

I turn and walk to the door as fast as I can.

I hope I'm strong enough to do this . . .

NICO ARRIVED ABOUT AN HOUR ago. Of course he is always down to do whatever I ask. It's been that way since the day I met him. It's nice having someone you can rely on.

"You want another beer, man?"

I tilt my head to look at Nico. He's standing by the fridge, dressed up in a black button down and dark jeans with his light hair styled back. He can hold his own when it comes to physical attributes. Getting girls is never a problem for him. I have no doubt that he won't please Onyx. The thought kills me, but I won't let it win and bring me down. I will smolder it on contact. She needs this. I need to give it to her, so maybe we can move on from the past. People like to say not to get even, but it's the only way to lay things to rest.

"Nah. I'm good."

My heart jumps to my throat when I see a car pull up in front of the house. I knew she would show. The question was when. It's already past three a.m. Not that it matters. She's here and that's what counts. It just gives me the confirmation that a part of her still wants me. Whether it's just physical, emotional, or both, I will find out soon enough. Time. Just a little more time.

A light knock sounds at the door, causing Nico to set his beer down and lift his eyebrows. "She's here, man."

"Yeah," I whisper to myself. "Let her in. Just remember what I said. Don't push the limits," I say firmly.

I walk to the bathroom and close the door behind me. This is going to be a lot harder than I thought. I'm already fighting the urge to crush Nico for touching her. I never was one for sharing. That's what makes it even harder knowing that she felt like she had to. Being sober makes it easy to feel what she must have, and brings it all forth to the light. I hate myself for always keeping her in the dark.

I take a deep breath and slowly exhale as I hear their voices in the distance. I can't make out what they're saying, but I can hear the tone in Nico's voice. He's getting himself ready and easing her in for what's to come.

"Fuck." I hit the sink before leaning into it and resting my head against the mirror. "Don't be a pussy. This is for her. She deserves this," I tell myself. I need to get this over with, and fast. No putting it off. It's time to get straight to the meaning of this visit and show her I'm willing to fight for her this time. No pussying out.

Pushing the door open, I walk through the hall to meet them in the living room. Onyx instantly spots me and freezes in her tracks. She looks stunning in her little black dress and heels. It's enough to take my breath away. The ink on her skin only adds to it, giving her a sexier edge now, which is my kind of woman; although, my kind has always only been her, and always will be.

She clears her throat and looks between Nico and me. She looks slightly nervous, but quickly shakes it off. "Well, I'm here, Hemy." She runs her fingers across the wall while making her way over to the couch, seductively. She looks over her shoulder at me. "Are you sure you can handle this?" The girl I knew four years ago is forever gone. I need to keep reminding myself. We are on a different game level now.

I swallow back my anger and focus all my energy on pleasing her. I just need to remember that she needs this to move on from the world of hurt I bestowed on her. She needs me to feel what she felt. "I can handle a lot of shit. Pleasing you is one." I nod my head toward Nico. "This is Nico. He's yours to do with as you please."

"Nico." She smiles while leaning against the back of the couch. "I like that name. Come here, big guy."

Nico looks at me in hesitation before I motion for him to go. The faster, the better, cause after this is done, she's staying with me. I don't care what it takes. She'll sleep in *my* bed and wake up in *my* bed.

Already knowing the plan, Nico walks over to stand in front of Onyx. He wraps one arm around her waist while fisting her hair and kissing her neck.

Onyx lets out a little moan as her eyes connect with mine. I hold her stare and bite my bottom lip as I nod my head for her to go on. I'm not surprised that she's a tad hesitant.

Grabbing onto the top of Nico's shirt, Onyx pulls him into her, causing them both to fall over onto the couch. His lips instantly seek hers as he buries himself between her legs and squeezes her bare thigh.

I walk over to the leather chair and take a seat in front of them. As much as I hate the thought of someone touching her, I can't help my cock from getting hard. The plan is to watch him touch her, taste her, and arouse her for a while before I join. It's how Nico always does it with me. Sitting here now, in his seat, I'm not sure how he does it.

"Take her dress off," I command.

Nico pulls away from the kiss and they stand, before he grabs the bottom of her short, tight, dress and eases it up her body, then pulls it over her head. "Fuck me," he growls out as he takes in her body.

I sit here, my eyes roaming over her tight little body as I grab my cock and rub it through the fabric. "Don't be shy, Onyx. This is what you wanted." I bite my bottom lip in anger. "Take his clothes off. Show me how it feels to be the viewer, witnessing the ultimate betrayal from someone you trust. Hurt me like I hurt you. My heart is yours to stomp on."

She looks at me, clearly struggling on the inside. I can tell she wants to see me suffer as much as she did, but a part of her hates having to hurt me. I have to push her more, or else she may just walk away for good. I can't live with that option.

85

"Remember those hands on my body, Onyx. Do you still visualize all of those girls touching me while I was high out of my fucking mind? How did that make you feel? Make me feel exactly how you felt."

Full of heated anger, she rips the front of Nico's shirt open and rubs her hands over his defined chest and abs with an animalistic growl.

"That's it, baby. Let it all out. Do this for you . . . do this for us." I grip the arm of the chair, biting back my anger as she goes for his jeans and tugs them off with force. He's standing there in only his briefs now.

"Touch her, Nico," I bite out. "Give her what she needs. Bend her over the couch and lick her pussy. You better fucking lick it good too."

Knowing I'm a pro at eating Onyx's pussy makes me smile to myself. There is no way she will enjoy it as much as when it's my tongue pleasuring her. Knowing that I'm here watching her will only make her realize that it can be me. All she has to do is ask.

Nico smirks while gripping Onyx's hips and pushing her down so that her hands are buried in the couch and her ass is up in the air. He squats, slowly pulling her panties down along the way, baring her pussy to both of us. My cock jumps at the sight and I have to fight the urge to run my tongue up it.

I watch as Nico positions on his knees, grips her firm ass, and runs his tongue up her slick folds. I glance down at Onyx's face to see her not looking the least bit impressed. It makes me smile on the inside, although, the bigger part of me wants to yank Nico away from her. She's supposed to be mine and mine alone, but I fucked that up.

Nico gets into it, shoving his tongue deep, pulling it in and out while pulling his briefs down and stroking his cock behind her. A little moan escapes from Onyx's mouth, but nothing compared to when I pleasured her.

"Hemy," she moans out. "I need you to get naked. Take those clothes off before I scream." She twists her neck to look at me in anticipation.

Smirking, I slowly unbutton my white shirt before ripping the last few buttons off and tossing my shirt aside. I stand and pull my belt through the loops, the leather sounding along the way. I unbutton my jeans, sliding down the zipper, slowly and teasingly.

Her eyes stay focused on me as I slowly pull my jeans down my body and step out of them. I'm not wearing any briefs, so I'm now standing here completely nude and hard, baring my whole body to her. I hear her suck in a breath as her eyes look me over, taking in every inch of my flesh, but mostly my hard as steel cock that gives away the effect she has on me.

Walking over to the couch, I stand beside her face, but at eye level. Her eyes follow her peripheral vision until she is staring directly at my rock hard cock before her. She licks her lips and moans as she takes me in. She always did like it rough.

"Damn, Hemy," she breathes. "I can't believe you're going through with this without killing someone. It fucking hurts, doesn't it? It killed me, Hemy. How the hell are you standing there and not choking someone?"

I grind my jaw, keeping in my anger. "Other people might not understand why I am willing to do this or why you would enjoy it, but fuck them. They never understood us in the first place and we have always been anything but normal," I whisper. "I'm doing this for you."

I stroke my cock close to her face as Nico devours her pussy from behind. "You like this, baby?" I step closer and rub the tip of my dick against her lips, causing her to tremble. "Remember how much you loved sucking my cock?"

She nods her head and lets out a little moan so I stroke it faster. I see her eyes zoned in on my piercings, letting me know she's imagining what it feels like to have them inside her. She won't be waiting for long. She'll be asking soon enough. I can see it in her eyes – all hooded.

I rub the tip of my cock across her eager lips again, but this time she opens them and slowly takes my length in, moaning out as it hits the back of her throat. Looking up at me, she swirls her tongue around my shaft and slowly trails it up toward the head, focusing on the piercings. I allow her to enjoy the taste of me for a few more seconds before pulling out, causing her to groan. That should be enough to make her want more.

Nico, still stroking his cock, slaps her ass before shoving a finger inside her pussy and moving in and out while moaning in pleasure. "You want my cock," he questions. "I can fuck you good for Hemy. You want that?"

Onyx looks up into my eyes before whispering, "No. I want yours, Hemy. I want you to fuck me while he watches. You're the only one that has been able to fuck me right. God, those piercings are so hot. What are you trying to do to me?"

Now that's what I like to hear. We always did have a good time and I can't help but to gloat at the fact that no man has ever been able to pleasure her like me. I also love that she mentioned the piercings. I knew she would love them.

"Back up, Nico," I command. "Stroke your cock for her while I fuck her. Don't come until she says so."

Nico stands up with his cock in his hand before walking over and taking a seat in the chair in front of the couch. This is exactly what we were both hoping for. Nico likes to watch as I put on a show. Having Onyx as the show is not what I hoped, but if it helps her move on, then I have to do it.

Walking behind Onyx, I push her face into the cushion and hold both of her legs up, gripping her thighs. This makes it easier to pound into her sweet little pussy from behind. Fuck, how I have missed the feeling of being deep inside her.

She may want me to go down on her first, but I'll save that for a different day since that's her favorite thing. I'm going to make this rough and deep to remind her of our wild sex life. That will only make her crave more and keep coming back until I can make love to her and make her mine again.

"No condom with me anymore, baby. I'm claiming this pussy as mine. I want to feel all of you as I pound into you." I grip onto the back of her hair with one hand and pull back. "Is this pussy mine?"

She moans out and her grip on the couch tightens. "Yes. Just fuck me. Stop with the teasing. You know we've both been waiting a long time for this."

"I know," I say firmly. "Now you're going to remember what it's like to have a real man inside you. Fuck all the boys in between. This is the real thing."

I adjust my cock at her entrance and gently slide into her while wrapping my arm around her neck. I bury it deep with one thrust, causing her to moan out and dig her nails into my arm. "Oh shit! It's so deep," she moans. "Hemy! I want to feel those piercings as you pound me. Fuck me like you used to. Please!"

Fuck! She feels so good . . . so warm and wet for me. I've never been inside her like this before and I can't help but to dwell on the fact that she didn't resist. She has to have been wanting me for as long as I have wanted her. We're both desperate for each other's touch but that's not going to be enough to stop her from guarding her heart.

"You miss screaming my name, don't you?" She nods her head as I pull her neck back. "You want to scream it for Nico?" I slap her ass and grip her thigh tighter. "This is just a taste of what you've been missing over the years. Hold on tight, baby."

I pull out and pound back into her with force while holding one leg up and gripping her neck with my other hand. "Oh God," she cries out. "Yes . . ."

"Scream my name and I'll give it to you harder. I'll make both you and Nico come at the same time. As soon as you tell him to go, you're both done for."

I pound into her with deep, fast movements, causing her to scream out my name. Being inside of her has me on a temporary high. This is better than any high I used to get in the past. This is the ultimate high. She's all I need.

90

I continue to thrust into her, stretching her tight little pussy to accommodate my huge size. She cries and screams with each thrust, causing Nico to stroke his cock faster.

Releasing her neck, I reach below us and rub my finger over her swollen clit while pulling her hair and pushing as deep as I can go, swaying my hips in and out in a fast rhythm.

Her screams become louder as I bite into her shoulder and moan out with her. I wish I could give her more right now, but this is what I need to do to keep her coming back and wanting more. I'll do whatever it takes. That's a fucking promise.

Holding her against my body, I swing her around so that her hands are on the floor and I'm holding her legs up as I continue to bury myself deep. I'm fucking her in a handstand, her fingers digging into the black carpet as she screams out. It feels so good from this angle. There is no doubt in my mind that she's about to come for me.

"Now, Nico," she cries out. "Fucking come! Please!"

Her head tilts to the side to watch as Nico strokes his cock a few more times before he's moaning out and shooting his cum into his palm.

Right before he's done, I pound into her one last time causing her body to convulse as she throbs around my dick, bringing me to climax along with her. I shoot my cum deep inside her tight little pussy before pulling out, flipping her around and slamming my lips against hers.

Her lips instantly react to mine as she tangles her fingers in my hair while panting and still shaking from her release. I always did love the feel of her panting in my mouth after she came. That hasn't changed. I love it just as much.

Fisting her hair, I place my forehead against hers and rub my hand up her back. "Stay with me tonight. I want you in my bed."

She gets ready to shake her head, but I pull her closer to me and pull her bottom lip into my mouth. She always loved that in the past. "I won't take no for an answer. Just for tonight. Let me run you a bubble bath and take care of you. You need to see me for who I am now."

She lets out a little breath before relaxing in my arms. She's silent for a few moments, lost in thought, before looking up at me. "Just for tonight, Hemy. After this, I have to be careful. This is it. I have no choice. This is pushing it. I should say no."

I look over at Nico as he stands up to get dressed. "Thanks, man. You can go now."

Nico smiles while wiping his hand off on his shirt and balling it up. "Not a problem, man." He grabs for his shoes. "I hope you two work shit out. That was some hot shit."

I turn my head away from Nico to look into Onyx's eyes. I want to see her reaction to his words. What I find is not good. She looks terrified. Being close to me scares the shit out of her. I need to change this.

And fast . . .

CHAPTER EIGHT

Onyx

I CAN'T BELIEVE I JUST let that happen. What was I thinking? Now, I'm really confused. I thought making Hemy watch me with another man would make me feel good. It didn't. It hurt. It made me feel sick to my stomach. I had to stop things before they got too far. The truth is, all I wanted was Hemy.

As much shit as Hemy put me through in the past, hurting him only hurts me more. How am I supposed to do this? How am I supposed to ever get over all the pain and suffering he put me through? I can never *be* with Hemy. All he does is hurt people. That's exactly why I need to see if he has changed before I tell him what I know. I have to be 100% positive first. I won't let him hurt anyone else like he hurt me.

I'm sitting on the couch wrapped up in Hemy's shirt when he walks out from the bathroom and runs his hand through his hair. It reminds me of how good it felt to run my hands through it and I can't help the butterflies in my stomach that are fluttering freely. "Hey," he says in a low, flat tone.

"Hey," I say back in the same voice level, not really sure what to do next. This feels so strange. Being with him again brings me back to the past, making me feel as if we were never apart.

"Come here." He reaches above him and grips the molding above him on the door. I can't help but to notice all of his muscles flex as his grip tightens. It's so damn sexy. "Take my shirt off. I need to see all of you. Never cover up around me."

He always did hate it when I wore clothes after sex. He said he couldn't sleep afterwards unless he had my naked body pressed against his. I learned very quickly to stop getting dressed after sex, because it was pointless. If I did he would just remove them himself. Sometimes when he was out at night, I would even lie in bed naked hoping it would help me sleep better. It never did.

Standing up, I grab the bottom of his shirt and pull it over my head. I stand here in place, watching his eyes scan over my body, before walking over to stand in front of him. I want him now that I've had another taste and I hate myself for feeling this way. I'm only going to get hurt. I was devastated for far too long, and I'm finally in control of my emotions, or I was.

Biting his bottom lip, he reaches out and cups my face in his hands. His eyes meet mine, causing my heart to speed up. They look clear again. A spark of hope shoots through my body, making me want to believe it's not a coincidence that he's been clean the last few times I have seen him. I want to believe he is telling me the truth.

He must notice me focusing on his eyes, because his lips turn up into a slight smile before he tilts my chin up and looks directly into my eyes. "I wasn't lying when I said I was clean. I will never lie to you. That's a promise I made ten years ago and I'll never break it."

"Hemy . . . I-"

"I know," he breathes, cutting me off before I can finish. "It's not that simple. If you just give me the chance I will show you." He swallows hard while tracing my bottom lip with his thumb. "I will *never* hurt you again. That is a fucking promise, baby. The day you walked away changed my perspective dramatically."

Before I can respond, Hemy scoops me up in his arms and carries me into the bathroom. He steps into the huge bathtub filled with bubbles and sits down, pulling me into his lap. I instantly rest my head back on his shoulder and sigh in contentment. He's never done this with me before. I'm going to soak this feeling up while I can, before I have to put my guard back up.

I should be keeping my distance, but maybe letting him in for one night won't be so bad. I mean, how much can really happen? It's just one night.

I close my eyes as I feel Hemy wrap his arms around me, underneath my breasts. His touch is so gentle, yet possessive; as if he's telling me I am his and his alone. The thought causes my heart to pound in my chest. The thought of being his gives me a feeling of warmth and safety, even though being with him in the past was anything but that.

"I'll take care of you if you let me," he breathes into my ear. "I may have only been rough in the past, but I promise you I can be gentle with you too. Things are different . . . I'm different. If you give me another chance to love you, I promise I will make you the happiest woman in the world. I don't need other women, Onyx. None of them are you. None of them took care of me when I was a broken boy, scared, and alone in the world. None of them took me in and held me at night after my parents left me and I lost Sage. That was the most devastating time in my life. Only you were there. Not even my foster parents cared for me. They let me do as I pleased and never gave a shit, but you did."

He takes a deep breath and squeezes me tighter, resting his chin on my shoulder. His hair brushes over my neck, causing me to shiver in his strong arms. I want to give into him, but I can't. *Damn, this feels so good; too good.* "I'm sorry I couldn't be there for you like you were for me. I just . . . I had to numb myself from the world. I had a constant storm of fucked up memories in my head that consumed me. I can't change the past, but I can promise you better for the future."

I can't help the tear that runs down my face. I still remember Hemy as the broken boy I met ten years ago. He was roaming down the alley behind my house with a group of older boys – all troublemakers. He stopped when he saw me and I couldn't help but to smile at him. He was the cutest boy I had ever seen and when he smiled back, a warm feeling enveloped me. After that day, I sat behind my house for at least a week waiting for him to walk by again. When he did, he walked over to me and I instantly wrapped him in a hug, surprising him. There was something about him that made me feel like he needed some tender care. I was right. He needed that and much more. After that, we were inseparable.

I let the tear roll down my cheek, being sure that it drips away from Hemy. I don't want him to know he's sparking some deep emotions inside of me. I have to be strong.

"Hemy," I whisper.

"Yeah." He pulls my hair back and holds it in a ponytail.

"I don't want to talk about us. Can we just enjoy this bubble bath without me having to hurt you? Please, I don't want to hurt you."

Letting out a small breath, he shifts so he can reach beside him and light the few candles that surround the tub. When his arms release me, a part of me feels dead inside. The feeling scares the shit out of me. I haven't even spent much time with him and I'm already dreading not being in his arms.

After lighting the candles, he grips my hips and turns me around so that I'm straddling his lap. I grip his shoulders and push away from him as he tangles his hands in my hair. "Hemy," I warn. "I need to be careful."

"There is no being careful when it comes to me," he says confidently. "I'm yours. I always have been. Nothing will ever change that."

His hands tighten in my hair and he grinds below me, digging his semi hard erection between my legs. The feel of the steel bars, poking me, make me want to jump on his cock and go for a ride – a Hemy ride.

I wrap my legs around his waist and close my eyes as he brushes his lips over my neck and shoulder. Being with him this way feels better than anything I have felt in years. I need a distraction, something to steer my thoughts in another direction.

"Do you still wonder about your sister," I ask, stopping his kisses. "Are you still looking for her?"

I feel his body tense below me before his arms wrap around my waist and pull me closer to him. "Every fucking day. It seems no one in Wisconsin is named Sage. Wisconsin was the last place I saw her before I was adopted and my foster parents moved me here to Chicago. I still check in, hoping that maybe she will pop up. No fucking luck. I have even checked anywhere within a few hours of Wisconsin and nothing. My parents were pieces of shits and did this on purpose. They left us in different places, Onyx. They dropped me off an hour away from home and then took off with Sage. I know they dropped her off too. Then they ran. No one has seen them since. They were miserable and wanted to be sure we would be too."

I take in a gulp of air at the reminder of how Hemy was left alone at such a young age. He lost his whole family; they never even cared to begin with. Sage was the only one he truly had and he couldn't even protect her from his parents' harm.

"Do you think you would know Sage if you saw her? I mean how would you know it was her? It's been ten years and she was so young."

His eyes go hard as his jaw ticks. He has so many bad memories that I hate even asking this.

"I may not recognize her right away, but I would know if I saw the back of her neck."

I reach behind his head and wrap my fingers in his hair for comfort. "From when your father burnt her with that pan?"

"Fuck!"

I jump away from his loud outburst, but he grabs me and pulls me back to him.

"I'm sorry." He grinds his jaw and closes his eyes. "Yes. That happened like two years before I lost her. We were all in the kitchen, waiting for my mother to finish the last bit of dinner. Sage was crying. She was hungry, because we hadn't eaten in over two days. I tried to comfort her, but she just kept crying and saying *Ty, I'm hungry* over and over again. Back then I didn't go by Hemy. My father hated my mother for naming me that. He made me go by my middle name." He stops and shakes his head. "Anyways. My father got tired of her crying so he picked her up by her arm and dragged her across the kitchen and over to the stove. He grabbed for the pan my mom was cooking on and held it against the back of her neck, smiling as she screamed out in pain.

"When I ran over to help her, my dad took the pan and swung it at my face, hitting me, and causing me to fall back and hit my head on the corner of the counter. I blacked out, and all I remember is waking up to Sage crying and sitting next to me on the kitchen floor while my parents were at the table eating without us. The pan left an odd shaped scar on the back of her neck. I'll always remember that mark."

I turn my head away and swipe at the tears as they begin to fall down my face. The thought of Hemy hurting kills me. All of a sudden, all I want to do is go to bed and get the night over with. I can't think anymore. I want to hold him while I sleep – one last time. Just this one night.

Hemy notices me crying and instantly reaches out to dry my tears. "Don't cry for my past. It only made me stronger. I may not have been strong four years ago, but I promise you now, that I will be the strongest man you know. Taking care of you is what will make me strong; protecting what I love the most in life."

My heart takes on an odd rhythm as I watch his face. All I see is truth in his words. He's never told anyone that he loves them, except Sage and although he didn't exactly come out and say it, it's the closest thing to it for him. It makes me want to hold onto him and never let him go.

I clear my throat and pull his hands away from my face. "It's getting really late and I'm tired. Can we just go to bed now?"

He looks my face over before smiling and rubbing under my eyes one last time. "Yeah. Let me put you to bed. It's late as shit."

He stands up and gets out of the tub. Reaching for a towel, he turns around and reaches for my hand to help me out of the water, before draping the towel over my shoulders. I stand here and watch as he blows the candles out and drains the water out of the tub.

"Next time we're in that tub, I'll be making love to you."

He grabs my hand and pulls me through the house, his body dripping wet as he guides us to his bedroom. Without turning on the light, he gets into his bed and tugs on the towel, pulling me down next to him.

"Lose this," he whispers while unwrapping me from the towel. "You know I can't sleep unless I'm wrapped up in your naked body."

I sit on my knees, naked, as Hemy takes me all in. Then, he pulls me down so that I'm lying down next to him. He leans over and presses his lips against mine, soft at first, before going rough and deep, causing us both to moan into each other's mouths. He kisses me for a few seconds longer, before moving down in between my legs, spreading them apart and kissing his name that is tattooed on the inside of my thigh.

My heart melts at the familiar feel, making it harder to fight my emotions.

"Goodnight, baby," he whispers, while lying back down and pulling me close to him.

I close my eyes and cuddle in next to him, feeling his naked body flush against mine. Man, it feels so, so good; too good.

"Goodnight," I whisper as his grip on me tightens.

Guarding my heart is going to be a lot harder than expected . . .

CHAPTER NINE
Hemy

I WAKE UP TO AN empty bed; the sheets smell of Jasmine and Vanilla. I always did love the scent of her hair. It always relaxed me, making me feel . . . alive. I've missed that scent almost as much as I have missed her.

Getting her to stay last night was a long shot; having her here in the morning was the impossible. I knew that from the beginning, but I learned to live with the idea and flowed with it. I just hope our night was enough to have an effect on her. If not, then I have a shit ton of work ahead of me.

Grumbling, I sit up and bury my hands in my hair. Having her next to me felt a lot better than I remembered. How can I ever live without that feeling now? She has ruined me. With her; I feel at peace. I feel like a real person. There is no way I'm giving up this fight, as much as I know she wants me to. A real man never gives up on his woman; he would die for her . . . and I would.

Sitting here; I feel empty. I don't have to work tonight so I need to find a way to keep my mind busy before I drive myself insane with thoughts of her.

"Shit! I need to do something."

I stand up, still naked and smelling of her. It instantly arouses me and I need a release. I make my way to the bathroom and run a cold shower; my thoughts stray back to her and the smooth curves of her body.

The ice cold water should be helping with my hard on, but it's not. It's so fucking hard, it's beginning to hurt. The only way to get rid of it, is to release the pressure. Placing one hand against the shower wall, I grip my cock, close my eyes and stroke it to the images of Onyx in my head.

Picking up speed; it doesn't take long before I'm busting my load into the water, it washing down the drain.

I stand under the frigid water for a few more minutes before quickly washing up, turning off the water and reaching for a towel. The doorbell rings, just as I finish wrapping the towel around my waist.

A spark of hope surges through me at the idea that it could be Onyx. Although the rational part of me already knows that it isn't. She said so herself that she needed to keep safe. The more she's with me; she's in danger of falling for me again and getting hurt. At least in her eyes; she thinks I'll hurt her. I don't blame her for being afraid.

Securing the towel, I make my way to the living room, crack open the shade and look out. I almost feel like punching something when I realize that it's only Stone outside. What the fuck could he want?

I yank the door open and give him a hard look. I can't really be mad at him, but I can't help but to be disappointed that I was right about it not being Onyx.

"What the hell are you doing here?" I growl while pushing my wet hair away from my face.

He smirks and slaps my shoulder, walking past me and into the house. "Nice to see you too, guy." He jumps over the couch and takes a seat. "Dude, this couch smells like sex."

Slamming the door shut, I walk over to stand behind the couch. "Yeah. Your hand is in my dried up cum right now. Now what the fuck do you want?"

My attitude doesn't even phase Stone. He's so used to my mood swings that he just brushes it off. He knows I mean no harm. That's one thing I like about this kid. He may only be twenty-one and a little inexperienced, but he's a pretty decent dude and doesn't take stupid shit to heart.

Lifting an eyebrow, he shrugs off my outburst. "Let's go out tonight. It's Cale's night to work. I have a place in mind that I want to go to but I need a partner." He pauses for a second to turn on the TV. *Sure, make yourself at home.* "There's a girl I want to see. I met her at that house we danced at last week. Her name is Ash. She's sexy as all hell but I'm trying to play it cool. I know she wants me, but I'm not giving this dick up that easy."

I think about it for a second and then I realize that this Ash girl probably works with Onyx. She might not like me showing up at her work again, but I don't give a shit. I will show up there every night until she gives me a second chance. That's how stubborn I am.

"Where?" I take my towel off and run it through my hair. "I might be down."

Stone turns around to look at me right as I wrap the towel back around my waist. "*Vixens Club,* man. I heard from one of the other girls that she works there. I've been thinking about going to see her for a while. You down?"

"Yeah," I say stiffly. "I'm down. Meet me back here around nine."

Standing up, Stone gives me a fist pound and heads for the door. "Alright, bro. I'm out."

"Cool."

I watch as Stone walks outside, forgetting to shut the door behind him. "Idiot," I mutter before walking over to shut it.

I stand here in thinking mode for a moment. This may make me sound like a pussy, but I want to be sure to look sexy as hell for her tonight. I'm going to dress this body of steel up for her and she won't be able to resist. I'm making it my mission to make her mine again.

WHEN NINE O'CLOCK ROLLS AROUND, I'm standing outside my house waiting on Stone to show up. I'm dressed in my favorite white button down, the sleeves rolled up to the elbows and the top few buttons undone, displaying my tats. I threw on a pair of dark fitted jeans that show off my muscular thighs, black boots and my hair is pulled back out of my face. Hell, I even trimmed my beard a bit to be sure it looks sexy for her.

Stone rolls up in his Jeep and whistles when I walk over and jump in the passenger seat. "Damn, dude. You trying to give the ladies a walking orgasm? You look studdish tonight." He reaches over and grabs the top of my collar, tugging slightly. "Damn, guy. I need to borrow that shirt sometime."

Shutting the door, I smirk slightly. "Come on, man. Stop creaming yourself over my clothes and let's go. No woman is going to want your ass if you walk in with nut stains."

"Fuck yeah, they would. Once I bust out my moves; the ladies can never resist." Stone lets out a satisfied laugh while grinding in his seat and pulling back out in the street and taking off. "No worries here."

We drive in silence for a few minutes, me lost in my own thoughts, trying to decide my best move for tonight before Stone interrupts me.

"You dressing up for someone? You never did tell me why you ran out of *Walk Of Shame* that night." He glances over at me and I grind my jaw at the thought of that night. I still can't get over what I found that night; her being in that place, rubbing all over that filth. She's too good for that shit. "I'm guessing it's for some fine ass girl. I've never seen your ass try before. Usually the grungy Hemy look is enough, my man."

"Yeah, man, not this time. Trust me," I reply. "It's for *the* girl. Not just any fucking girl. And she works with this Ash chick so don't make a fool out of yourself around me. I need to prove to her that I'm a different person. I'm taking it easy on shots and all that hard shit. Got it?"

Nodding his head, he pulls up to *Vixens Club,* parks the Jeep and kills the engine. "Sure thing, man. I've been there once. Good luck is all I can say. Once a woman sees all your fuck ups, it's hard for them to see you for the good. That shit stays with them forever."

My jaw ticks from his words as I stare up at the neon sign in deep thought. It just reminds me that there's a huge chance that Onyx will never forgive me for all the shit I put her through. Doesn't matter. It won't stop me from trying.

"Come on, man. Let's go."

I jump out of the Jeep and slam the door behind me, with Stone hopping out right after. I didn't mean to close it to the point of almost breaking it, but I can't seem to control the negative thoughts swarming through my head. The thought of not having her as mine makes me want to slam my fist through something.

"Take it easy, dude." Stone flares his nostrils while looking his Jeep over for any damage. "Don't take it out on my shit. Save it for the assholes in the bar."

"My bad," I growl. "I'll buy you a new one if I fucked it up. Let's just get this over with."

We reach the door and some guy made of muscles with a bald, shiny head and long beard about six foot five comes over and asks for Stone's ID. He gets ready to ask for mine but after getting a glimpse of my face, decides against it and just waves us past.

"Seriously, dude?" Stone complains. "Is it because of my handsome baby face?" He rubs his hand over his face as if he's all smooth and shit.

I give his dumb ass a push as the bouncer gives him a blank look while crossing his arms. "Real men have beards. Grow one," I say annoyed.

After getting past the bouncer, we quickly order a couple drinks and take a seat in the far back. The club is fairly busy tonight and the thought of having all these creeps' eyes on my girl is driving me mad.

I know she hasn't danced yet because the bartender said there are a couple more girls before her. I don't really care to watch the show. Onyx is the only one I came to see. Until then, I'm invisible in the background.

Sipping back a Gin and Tonic, Stone pulls out his wallet and sets it on the table. "This club is pretty damn nice. A hell of a lot nicer than ours." He runs his hand over the table in front of us while admiring it. "Black glass tables, red suede chairs and look at that stage. That's a sweet ass stage. I wonder if they'll let me dance here. You know," he smirks confidently, "To help bring them some more cash in."

I tilt back my beer and block Stone out. I haven't been this fucking nervous since before I hit fucking puberty. All I can think about is thrashing all the men in this room. I saw the way that piece of shit handled her last time I was here and it makes my blood boil that I didn't kick the shit out of him.

I take a look around the room, taking in all the assholes waving money around and screaming out like pigs. This must be the image Onyx has of me in her mind. I'm just like every one of these assholes. Until I can change that; that's what she sees.

Taking a long swig of my beer, almost finishing it off, I slam it down on the table and look over at Stone.

He's too zoned in on the entertainment on stage to even notice me standing up. "I'll be back."

Walking away with a quickness, I make my way back over to the bar and call for the bartender to come over. The beautiful blonde that helped us when we walked in, lifts her eyebrows and adjusts her tiny top while walking my way.

"Can I help you with something," she looks me up and down while playfully biting her lip, "big guy? You're looking awfully sexy to be here alone."

I ignore her sorry attempt to get my interest and pull out my wallet, prepared to make this shit happen my way tonight. "How much would it cost to get one of the girls to dance for me in a private room instead of on stage?"

The girl looks me up and down while leaning over the counter and reaching for my collar. "Why would you want to pay for one of these girls to dance for you when you can get *any* girl for free?"

"How much?" I growl out, pulling away from her touch. She gives me a confused look. "If you don't know then ask your manager. I need to know and quickly."

She takes a step back, her cheeks turning slightly pink with embarrassment. She clears her throat. "Umm. Well, we don't get that happening very often. If they're set to dance on stage then they usually can't do private dances until they're through. It's all on a schedule to fill the time."

Aggravation takes over as another girl enters the stage, swaying her hips wearing next to nothing. Onyx is next and I don't have time for games. I'll pay whatever the hell they want. I could care less about the money.

"Tell your boss I'll pay three grand to have Onyx dance for me in private. I'm sure he wouldn't mind the extra cash. Just make it happen."

The girl holds up her finger before walking over to the phone and making a call. She comes back a minute later and points down the hall. "The room all the way to the back. It's our biggest room and it gives you some privacy in case you don't want to be seen by the dancer. Roman said he'll make it happen. I'll give Onyx the message."

I turn to walk away, but stop before taking a step. "Do me a favor and don't describe me to her."

She nods in understanding so I turn and walk away.

Hope she still likes surprises . . .

CHAPTER TEN

Onyx

HALF ASLEEP, I FIGHT TO stay awake while finishing up my makeup. As much as I don't want to be here tonight, I'm up next on stage and I really don't have much of a choice. A huge part of me wanted to call in tonight, but the other part of me knows I can't let my emotions get in the way of earning my bill money. Still, I'm just so . . . exhausted.

I crawled out of Hemy's bed around eight this morning and left while he was too deep in sleep to take notice. I knew I had to get out of there before he woke, or else he would've somehow talked me into spending the whole day with him. I couldn't let that happen. The more he brings up the past and shows me how different he is, the more I want to give in and trust him. It's too soon for that.

After I got back to my own bed, I thought I would be able to get some rest, but I couldn't shut my mind off enough to fall back asleep. I ended up spending most of the day cleaning a house that was already clean and watching stupid TV shows, hoping they would wear me down enough to sleep. No luck there.

Tossing down my eyeliner, I look over to see if Ash is dressed and ready to go. She's up for her set on stage after me. I met Ash about a year ago, before I moved back home. We hit it off really fast and after she explained how she was tired of her dull life and her parents smothering her, I thought maybe it would be nice to bring her home with me and let her live a little.

I really had no idea what the hell I was going to do for a job, but then an old friend of mine told me about *Vixens* needing a couple dancers. I mentioned it to Ash and in her rebellious state she was down for it, and ready to have a little fun. Plus, knowing that I was going to be so close to Hemy kind of made me want to rebel a bit myself. I needed a hard exterior to make me seem less vulnerable. It worked for a while.

"You still like this job, Ash?" I ask, now questioning my decision to bring her here.

Smiling, she sets down her red lipstick and uncrosses her legs. "Yeah, for now. It's not a bad place. Plus, the money is way better than working some dead end waitressing job." She shrugs. "Might as well have a bit of fun while I'm still young."

I return her smile and then look beside us as the door opens and Kylie rushes in. She gives me a not so pleasant look and rolls her eyes. "There's been a change of plans. You're not going to be dancing on stage tonight."

Standing up, I place my hands on my hips and give her an equally disgusted look. Kylie usually seems to be friendly, but right now, I feel like slapping that smug look off her pretty little face.

"And why the hell is that?"

Mumbling under her breath, she tosses me a wad of cash and I reach out, barely catching it. "I can't believe Roman agreed to this, *but* someone paid a shit ton of money to have you do a private dance instead. Roman told me to give you a grand to do it." She turns and starts heading back for the door. "The sexy asshole is waiting in room ten. You probably shouldn't keep him waiting. Damn asshole," she mutters and leaves the room.

I hold up the wad of cash and bite my bottom lip in thought. I feel a rush at the thought that Hemy could very well be that sexy asshole waiting on me. The problem with that is I wouldn't expect him to pay a ton of money for me to dance for him when he knows he can practically get anything he wants. He always did . . . until I left him.

Just as quickly as I let the thought consume me, I push it away and take a deep breath. I guess if anything, it's still better than being on stage. I still can't get used to dancing for a room full of men. I seem to do better one on one. Plus, it's easier to stay in command when you only have one asshole to deal with.

Handing the cash to Ash, I force a smile. "Mind putting that away for us? Looks like I have a sexy asshole waiting for a show."

We both laugh as I start backing away.

"Seems like a pretty generous asshole at least." She lifts a brow and waves the cash. "Tell him thanks from the both of us. I'll be lucky to make half that on stage."

GATHERING MY THOUGHTS, I TAKE my time walking to room ten. If this asshole was desperate enough to pay the amount of money this had to have cost, then he's desperate enough that he'll wait and still enjoy it when I get there.

Walking past the main room, I see it's almost filled to capacity now. The music is loud, the men are loud, and the flashing lights make it harder to concentrate on what's on stage. I guess the strobe effects and beat of the music make it more exciting for the men, and to make them feel they have to fight in order to see the half naked girls swaying before them. It keeps them around longer, wanting to see more. That's what Roman thinks, at least. I think it's annoying as shit.

I make it down the hall and stop directly in front of the door, labeled with the number ten, staring for a moment before pushing the door open and stepping inside. I close the door behind me and try not to pay attention to who is in the room.

Room ten is the biggest private room we have. It's used for rich clients that want to remain discrete and don't want their faces shown to the public. Off in the back of the room, there's a huge leather chair for the client to relax in, and a light switch, giving them the option of showing their face or not. Lucky for me, this client wants to be kept a secret. It makes it easier to dance when I don't have to look into the creepy eyes that are glued to my every move. It's hard to be sexy when you feel so damn gross sometimes, as if the filth is sticking to you just by being in the room.

Pushing all thoughts aside, I walk past the darkened corner, taking long, smooth steps, and swaying my hips on my way up to the stage. The music is already playing a slow, sexy song; perfect for getting aroused to.

Standing with my back against the pole, I bring one arm back to wrap around it, and slowly lowering my body down the pole, while rubbing my other hand down the center of my body, over the white lace. Once I get close to the ground, I spread my knees apart and lower my hand some more, biting my bottom lip, seductively.

I sway my hips to the rhythm of the music, releasing the pole, and wrapping my hands in my hair, tugging as I make my way back up the pole in a stance. I make sure to look in the direction of the darkened corner to verify to the client I'm indeed dancing for his pleasure and his alone. This usually helps me get additional tips on top of what I already get for doing the private dance.

Slowly turning around, I wrap one leg around the pole and arch my back, swinging my wild hair around, before gripping the pole and spinning around it. I spin around a few times, moving seductively to the music, before releasing the pole, walking to the edge of the small stage, and reaching for the ribbon that's holding my corset together.

Pretending as if I'm looking directly in the mysterious guy's eyes, I lower myself to the surface of the stage, down to my ass, and spread my legs wide apart, revealing the sheer lace that's in between. I slightly tug the ribbon, opening my top a little more, and rolling my hips up and down with my back pressed against the stage.

I'm lost in my own little world, hoping to get this guy off, when all of a sudden I feel two hands grip my thighs and pull me to the edge of the stage. Out of instinct, I swing one leg up and wrap it around the guy's neck, squeezing.

I expect for whoever it is to let go of my thighs and apologize, but to my surprise, I get a growl and a bite on the inside of my thigh.

I recognize the growl right away, and I can't help the reaction that my body gets from it. My heart jumps to my throat and my whole body trembles with pleasure.

Another soft bite causes me to open my eyes to the sight of Hemy standing there, his hair pulled back, and his deep amber eyes set on me. His grip on my thighs tightens as I release his neck and lean my head back with my hands in my hair.

"Fucking shit, Hemy," I bite out. "You scared the shit out of me. What are you doing here? I told you-"

"Shhh . . ." he whispers against my thigh. "Don't talk. I'm not here for that. I'm here to taste my pussy and remind you of what is mine."

Before I can think of a response, my panties are pushed aside and Hemy moans out while running his thick finger over my slick folds. My body instantly reacts to his touch, causing me to moan out and bite my lip.

"You miss my mouth owning your pussy? It craves my tongue, doesn't it, baby?" He runs a hand down my thigh while shoving a finger deep inside me, causing me to grip the stage. "Tell me how bad you want me to taste you," he demands.

I look up at him, now getting a bit angry at him for making me admit it first. He's doing this to see how badly I want him. It makes me want to slap him and then ride the shit out of him. He always had that effect on me.

"Maybe I don't want you to," I whisper, looking up to meet his stare. "Maybe someone else has already claimed what was once yours." I can't resist but to push him back. One of us is bound to cave first.

Pulling my body up higher, he softly blows on my swollen clit while pushing his finger in and out. "You'll always be mine, Onyx." He squeezes my thigh and rubs his bottom lip up my heat, causing me to moan out silently. "This pussy . . . will always be mine. I claimed it six years ago when I made you my girl, and nothing has changed since."

He runs his lip up my pussy again, teasing me with his lip ring. I'm fighting so hard to resist, but I can't help it. Seeing Hemy dressed up, makes me want to have an orgasm right on the spot. *Feeling* his mouth on me almost has me exploding beneath him.

I thrust my hips upward, silently begging for him to lick me. He laughs against my throbbing clit before reaching up with one hand and grabbing my left breast. His dominance has me on the verge of explosion and I want to feel this to its full extent.

"I want to feel your tongue on me so damn bad," I blurt out, thrusting my hips again to meet his mouth. "Remind me of how good it feels. Now."

With a cocky smile, Hemy grips my ass with both hands and pulls my hips up to meet his face. Looking at me with pure heated desire, he runs his tongue, slowly and teasingly, up my wetness, causing me to shake uncontrollably in his arms.

He rubs circles around my clit with his tongue, before trailing it back down my folds and pushing it into my entrance. This causes me to wrap my legs around his head and squeeze. I can't seem to get him close enough and he knows this. He knows my weakness and is using it against me to get me where he wants me. It's working and I hate him for it.

The better it feels the angrier I seem to get, until finally, I growl out and pull away from him. At least, I try to. He catches my legs and pulls me off stage so that I'm straddling his narrow hips. With a smile, he walks us both up the stairs and up to the stage.

He stops in front of the pole, turns my back toward it, and presses me against it, breathing in my ear. "Hold on tight." With little effort, he lifts me up, causing me to reach behind me and grip onto the pole at a higher level. Before I can wonder what he's doing, he rests my thighs on his shoulders, grips my waist, and buries his face in my pussy.

His tongue works like magic, owning my pussy just like in the past. My whole body trembles from the heat of his mouth and the feel of his tongue tasting me, slowly and teasingly.

He reaches up with one hand and rubs his thumb over my clit, while working his tongue, rough and fast, speeding up to get me off. My grip on the pole tightens as he shoves his tongue back inside just in time for me to come.

I shake on his shoulders for a few seconds, high off the release of my orgasm. It feels so damn good I can almost cry in relief. Releasing the pole, he pulls me away from it and slowly lowers me down his body, kissing me in different places along the way. It doesn't take much for him to lower me back down to my feet and press his body into mine.

Looking into my eyes, he cups my face and runs his tongue over his lips in satisfaction. "I want you back at my place tonight." I shake my head, but he stops me by pressing his lips against mine, claiming my lips as his. The kiss is rough and possessive, and I can't help but to get turned on again.

After a few moments pass, he pulls away from the kiss and turns to walk away without another word. My whole body screams for me to run after him, but I can't. I'm stuck in place, trying to figure out how I let him take control of me again.

Screw this. I'm letting him know that he doesn't control me. He hasn't in a long time. He has no say whether or not I go to his place and stay with him. He lost that say years ago.

Making sure that I'm covered, I rush out of the room and walk down the dark hallway. I stop when I get to the main room and look around in search of him. It doesn't take long to point him out. With Hemy looking as sexy as he is tonight, it's hard to miss him.

He's standing next to a table with another guy. I recognize him from Jade's party. He's one of the three strippers that danced that night. I recognize the black hair and tattoos. Realizing that he must be here to watch one of the girls, my gut tells me to get Hemy out of here.

He might assume I'm giving into him, but I'm really just trying to preserve my secret a bit longer. He *seems* different, but I'm still scared.

Clearing my head and coming down from my temporary high, I walk over to the table, stopping in between him and the other guy. I place my hand on Hemy's chest and can't help the moan that slips out of my mouth. Just touching him has me all worked up.

"Wait for me outside. I'll go grab my things and meet you by your truck."

Biting his bottom lip, he grabs both of my hands and runs them up his chest, before pulling them up to wrap around his neck. He presses his body flush with mine and gives me a hooded look. "I don't have my truck. We'll take my motorcycle."

I smile at the memory of when the bike was his. After a while, he gave up on it and got a new one. I couldn't leave without it, because it brought back too many memories. I needed it as my safety net. I needed it to fall back on when I missed him too much, so after I packed my things and left that night, I sent my brother to pick up it up from storage. I made it mine with the memories of him.

"You mean my bike?" Smirking, I turn around in his arms and walk away, making him release me. If I know Hemy still, he'll be outside as soon as I'm out of sight.

After quickly grabbing my things and changing, I make my way outside to see Hemy leaning against my bike. Seeing him standing in front of it causes my heart to clench in pain. It brings back too many memories of us as teens, me holding on tightly as he learned how to ride it. It didn't take long and I always trusted him to keep me safe; a part of me still does.

He sees me approaching and walks over, placing the helmet on my head. "Give me the keys," he orders.

I think about it for a second and almost consider making him ride on the back, but that would just look too weird to even enjoy. Hemy is definitely too dominant for that. Alpha male is what he'll always be. Shit, it's such a turn on.

I toss him the keys without a fight, pull my helmet on, and put my backpack on. My black boots dig into the gravel as I hop on the back and watch as Hemy jumps on the front.

I don't know how much more of this I can take while guarding my heart.

I need to figure something out and fast . . .

CHAPTER ELEVEN

Hemy

THE FEEL OF HER ARMS wrapped around my waist brings me back to the past. After I learned how to ride this motorcycle for the first time, she spent almost every day on the back of it, the two of us just riding to forget. Those are some of my happiest memories.

I can tell she's thinking about it too, because she hasn't said a word since we left the club, and not to mention that her arms are practically squeezing the life out of me. She always did that unintentionally in the past when she was deep in thought, and man does it feel good. This is exactly what I was hoping for. If I want another chance with her, then I'll have to remind her of the good stuff.

Riding past my block, I make a turn down the street that leads to Mitch's shop. Mitch's family has owned *Greenler's Mechanics* his whole life. Onyx and I spent a lot of time in it, playing and fooling around, when I was working on my motorcycle or showing off my mechanic skills to get her worked up. She always did have a thing for a dirty, hardworking man. I'm sure that hasn't changed much. At least, I can only hope.

Onyx doesn't bother looking up until we are already pulling up to the shop and parking. I can tell from her lack of smartass remarks. That, and I can feel her chin resting against my back. I don't think it's intentional, but I would dare say a word at the risk of her moving it. I feel her grip loosen as she lets out a little surprised breath. "Seriously, Hemy?" She releases my waist as I kill the engine. "Why would you bring me here? I thought we were going to your place."

Not bothering to respond, I help her off the bike and watch as she walks up to the building and stands there in silence. She probably hasn't even thought about this place in over four years. Bringing her here is sure to get the memories flowing in. It has to. I'm counting on it. Hell, I'm having a hard time just being here with her. I could do it alone over the years, but having her here makes my chest ache. It always will until she's mine again.

Grinding my jaw and pushing back my emotions, I grab Onyx's hand and pull her along with me as I walk around to the back and pull out my key. I've been meaning to work on my Harley for a while now, but I've been so damn busy working on other projects for Mitch that I haven't been able to touch it. It's about time I get my baby running good.

I push the door open and flip on the light. I feel Onyx's hand squeeze mine, and then she lets go and steps inside. "I haven't thought about this place in years, Hemy." She looks around, her face void of emotions. "It looks exactly the same." She cracks a smile. "As a matter of fact, I think you guys are still working on the same vehicles too."

I let my own smile take over as I watch her laugh at her own joke. Damn, her laugh is just as beautiful as ever. I never could get enough of that sound.

I step up beside her and nudge her with my shoulder. She looks up at me. "I love that sound," I say softly.

She looks around as if listening for something. "What sound?"

"When you laugh," I say honestly. Her smile fades as I look down into her eyes and then walk away.

I keep on walking, making my way to the back where my motorcycle is parked. It doesn't take but a few seconds before Onyx is standing right behind me. She's so close that I can feel the warmth from her body. I can sense her eyes studying me as I stand here.

"Why are we here?" she finally asks.

"I need to work on my bike. Why else would we be here?"

"It's like midnight. Don't you ever sleep?"

"Not anymore. I told you, I can't sleep for shit without you naked and next to me." I walk away, unbuttoning my shirt, before pulling it off and setting it on the closest car.

I kneel down in front of my Harley and reach for my tools. Onyx watches me in silence for a few seconds before she drops her bag down beside her and takes a seat on the hood of the car next to her. "I've kind of missed this, you know." She pauses and waits for me to respond, but I don't. I want her to keep going. "You working on your bike here and me watching. Us laughing and talking. I miss you like that."

I continue to work on my bike, not looking back at Onyx. "You always made it hard to get any work done. Your smell alone was enough to arouse me, but when you would undress behind me, sitting on a car . . ." My words trail off and I smirk to myself, knowing by the sound of her breathing that she's reliving the memories.

"What," she breathes. "Don't stop there, Hemy."

"All I could think about was burying myself deep between those thighs." I stand up, drop my tools, and walk over to stand between her legs. Placing my hands on her thighs, I trail my hands up them. "*My* thighs. All I wanted to do was to own your little pussy and release myself so deep inside you that I would ruin you for anyone else."

Her breathing picks up as I spread her legs and step between them. "Mmm . . . and I wanted you deep inside me. I never could watch you getting dirty without wanting you to get me dirty. Funny how that works." She leans forward and runs her tongue over my mouth, her tongue lingering on my ring before sucking my lip along with it into her mouth. "You were so damn sexy working on your bike that my clothes practically fell off. That look you made when concentrating on your work. Oh shit, I'll never forget that look."

I tangle my fingers in the back of her hair and look down at her with a serious look of concentration, imitating what she just described. It's not all just an act. I'm taking my time and concentrating on every last inch of her beauty. I bite my lip as she closes her eyes and breathes in. I know I have her. "This one," I question, stepping in closer to press my erection between her thighs.

Her body jerks from below me as I grind my hips a little. "Oh God, yes." She opens her eyes and takes in my face, her eyes filled with lust. "That one, exactly. Why are you doing this, Hemy? You knew this would happen if you brought me here. We can't keep doing this. I can't let myself fall in love with you again."

"You falling back in love with me is the *only* thing I want." Gripping her hair tighter, I crush my lips against hers, owning her lips, breath, and taste. Everything that she is right now is mine and I intend on keeping it this way. I'm taking this moment and owning it.

Her lips instantly part, allowing me entrance just like in the past. Everything about this moment brings me back to four years ago, and it only makes me want her more. Pulling back, I breathe against her lips, my hands still tangled in her hair. "You taste so damn good, baby." I bring one hand down and rub my thumb over her cheek before trailing down and over her bottom lip. "Seeing you up on the hood of this car makes me want to take you right here." I kiss her neck and make my way up to her ear, stopping to whisper. "Do you want that, baby? Huh? You want to remember what it was like, me taking you here, me all dirty and sweaty?"

"No," she whispers, pushing on my chest. "That's the last reminder I need, Hemy."

Grabbing her chin, I force her to look up into my eyes. I can tell by her heavy breathing and fidgeting that she's lying. She always did have a hard time hiding her feelings from me. "Dammit, Onyx. Don't lie to me. Tell. Me. The. Truth."

She nods her head, her breathing picking up as she reaches up to let my hair down. She looks lost in thought for a moment before she speaks. "You have no idea how sexy your hair is. Every time I look at you, all I can think about is gripping onto it as you make love to me."

My heart beats wildly in my chest, but then sinks to my stomach as she turns her head away in shame. She does that when she says something she didn't mean to. Every part of me wants her to mean those damn words. I may not have made love to her in the past, but things have changed. I've changed. I'm willing to give her anything she wants.

I pull her face back to mine and bring my lips down to hover over hers, our heavy breathing mingling together. "If you give me a chance," I bring my eyes up to meet hers," I'll make love to you. I'm capable of more than you think now, Onyx."

She stares at me for a second, not saying a word, before a small smile creeps over her face. "Well, not tonight." She grips my hair and pulls on it roughly. "Tonight, I want you to fuck me like you did four years ago." She yanks my hair harder before releasing it. "Show me the old Hemy. *My* Hemy."

Her words set me off and before she can register what I'm doing, I have her back pressed against the hood of the car and her pants in my hands, yanking them down her legs. Kissing the inside of her thigh, I pull her boots off and toss them, before tossing her tight little jeans next to them.

I spread her legs further and kiss my way up to her stomach while reaching for her white tank top. "Fuck, Onyx." I love the way she looks laying across the hood of a car. I nibble my lip ring while pulling her shirt above her head and reaching behind her to release her bra. I take a few seconds to admire her body before gripping her thong in my hand and pulling her body into mine. Nothing is standing in the way of being inside her now but my jeans and her tiny lace thong. It's exactly like it was when we first fell in love. It's just too bad she never knew it.

Twisting her panties in my hand, I rip them off, the white lace coming untied with little effort. Onyx lets out a moan and arches her back as I lace one arm beneath her and bite down into her shoulder. "Oh God, Hemy," she pants. "Hurry up and get those jeans off."

Smiling against her neck, I work on taking off my jeans with one hand, while reaching down with my other to rub circles over her swollen clit. "Mmm . . . you're so wet for me, baby." I slide my jeans down my legs and let them drop, before spinning Onyx around and slamming her down onto the hood, grabbing the back of her hair.

"Spread your legs, baby." I lean down next to her ear and growl as she bites my arm. "Show me how bad you've missed me inside you."

She bites me harder, causing me to squeeze her left ass cheek before slapping it. She cries out with pleasure as I slap it one more time before gripping her ass with both hands and spreading her cheeks. "It's so damn beautiful," I whisper, while running a finger up her slick folds. "Hold on, baby. I'm about to take you for a ride."

Gripping my cock, I align it with her opening, rubbing the head of it over her slickness, teasing her with my piercings before shoving it deep inside with a moan. Holding onto her hips, I pound into her hard and fast, causing her to grab onto the hood and scream. The faster I go, the more she begs for me to go harder.

Grinding my hips, I yank her hair back with one hand, pushing hard and deep. I want her to still be able to feel me inside her after we're through. I want her to know she's mine and mine alone. I may have shared her once, but that'll never happen again.

She sticks her ass up higher, gripping onto my hand as I thrust into her. I'm already as deep as I can go and she still wants me deeper. We never could get enough of each other, even when it hurt her.

A few thrusts later, I feel her clenching around my cock, so I give her one hard thrust before yanking her neck to the side and pressing my lips against hers, right as she moans out. I wait for her to stop shaking before I pull out and spin her around to face me.

I crush my lips back against hers, both of us breathing heavy, as I pick her up and walk until we're pressed against the wall in our favorite corner. It was where we went to fuck when Mitch's ass wouldn't leave for the night. Even though he could still hear us, it kept us hidden pretty well in the shadows. The risk of getting caught made it more of a rush.

Pulling away from her lips, I wrap my hand around her throat and push myself inside her, causing her to shake in my arms. "Remember this spot, baby?" I pull her bottom lip into my mouth and bite into as I start thrusting hard and fast, pushing her up the wall with each movement.

I reach down and grab her hands, binding them in one hand, and raising them above her head. Both of us are breathing heavy, me holding her hands above her head while holding her up with my opposite arm supporting her waist.

"Hemy!" She pulls back on my hair as I push into her one last time, feeling my orgasm build before I release myself deep inside her.

We stand here, me holding her and her holding onto me as we fight to catch our breath. Lowering her back to her feet, I tangle my fingers in her hair and press my forehead against hers. "I fucking love you," I breathe out. "I love you so much that it hurts."

Sucking in a breath of shock, she places both her hands on my chest and shoves me away. "Damn you, Hemy!" Rushing over to her clothes, she struggles to get dressed while muttering under her breath and holding back tears.

I don't blame her for her reaction. I hurt her beyond words, and me dropping the L word like this was probably the last thing she expected . . . but I don't give a shit. I love her and she needs to know, no matter how much she hates me. I missed my chance the first time. It won't happen again. I'll never lose her again because I couldn't tell her how I felt.

I feel my heart shattering in my chest as she throws on her boots and reaches for her bag. As much as I know she needs to go, I don't want her to. She heads for the door, but then stops to turn around and throw something. Whatever it was hits the wall before she buries her face in her hands and shakes her head.

"Do you even know what pain feels like, Hemy?" Her jaw clenches as I stare at her. "Well, do you? Do you even feel pain?"

"Oh, I feel it alright. That burning sensation deep down inside that feels as if my heart is dying, being crushed." I look up from the ground and right into her eyes. "I felt it the minute you walked out my damn door."

She stands there, unable to say anything, before turning around and walking out the door, slamming it closed behind her. I have no one to blame but myself. I did this to her . . . to us.

It just means I need to work harder to show her the new me.

CHAPTER TWELVE

Hemy

IT'S BEEN FOUR DAYS SINCE I've seen Onyx and it's taking everything in me not to go to *Vixens'* and claim her as mine. As much as it hurts, she needs time. Me forcing her to admit her feelings isn't going to do shit but make it worse on my part. I can't have that.

Taking a drag of my cigarette, I tilt my head back up to look at Slade. He's puffing on his own cigarette while texting Aspen. "You love her, man?"

Slade gives me a hard look before shoving his phone in his pocket and taking one last drag of his cigarette before tossing it. "With everything in me," he says with confidence. "There's not a thing I wouldn't do for that woman."

I can't believe I'm even doing this right now. Going to Slade for advice was the last thing I thought I'd ever do. "What would you do if you hurt her so bad in the past that she was afraid to open up and let you back in?

What if you told her you loved her for the first time and she walked away?"

Taking a step closer to me, he grips my shoulder and smirks. "My guy's in love. This must be one badass chick." He shoves my shoulder before placing me in a headlock and rubbing the top of my head. "You've been holding out on me, my man."

I take one last drag of my cigarette as he releases my neck. "Yeah, she's badass. She's my first and only love, man. I fucked up bad and I'm paying for it now." I toss my cigarette and take a deep breath before quickly releasing it. "I'm trying to be patient, man. It's been four days and I haven't heard shit." I steel my jaw while leaning into the building and digging my fingers into it. "How much time should I give her?"

Without hesitation, he answers, "You know me, man. When I want something I go after it, sometimes a little too hard. If it's love, then you need to let her know that you're not going anywhere. Let her know you want her without pushing her away. You get me?"

I nod my head, getting what he means. I can still let her know I'm not going anywhere without being too pushy. My shift is almost over for the night, so as soon as I'm out, I'm going straight to *Vixens'*.

"Hemy."

We both look over at the sound of Sarah's voice. "The group dance is up next. You better hurry and get your fine ass in there." She smiles at Slade before shoving his shoulder. "Your woman is at the bar waiting on you. You better hurry before someone else snags her sexy ass up."

Oh boy. She just had to go there.

Without hesitation, Slade stalks off, rushing inside to his woman. He knows damn well he has nothing to worry about with Aspen, but he's still so damn protective. He reminds me a lot of myself. When we find that special woman, we'll do anything for her. I just wish I wasn't too late.

"Thanks, Sarah."

"Yeah, yeah. Just hurry your ass up," she teases.

IF THERE'S ANYTHING THAT I hate, it's doing a stupid dance routine on stage. It involves costumes and all of us men putting a dance together. It makes us all feel like fucking idiots. That's why we only set up a dance routine once a month. It's the one thing that some of the women travel to see. It's the biggest night of every month, packed to maximum capacity.

Adjusting my tie, I laugh at Stone as he jumps up on a table and thrusts his hips while gripping onto his hat and tilting it down, over his face. "Man, I'm such a stud in a suit."

"Is that right, asshole?" Cale asks.

"Um . . . fuck yeah," Stone replies while jumping down from the table. "Don't get mad when I get all the tips. I have this routine down pat, bros."

"Alright, *stud*." I slap the back of his head before reaching for my black hat and putting it on, tilting it a bit to the side. "This is the biggest crowd you'll see for a while, so you better show them Slade's not around anymore. A lot of them come just for that motherfucker."

"I'm the new Slade," he says with a smirk. "These women will leave screaming Stone. You feel me?" He gives both Cale and I the middle finger before jogging up the steps to the back of the stage.

This kid really has no idea what he's getting into right now. Some of these women still even scare my ass with all that shrieking.

The stage is dark when we line up next to our chairs. I can hear the screaming of hundreds of women as soon as the music starts playing. This used to get me hard at one point. Undressing for all these horny women. Now, I don't feel shit. I just want to get this over with.

Out of instinct, my body instantly reacts to the music when the lights flicker on, lighting up the stage. Placing one foot on the chair, I grab the top of my head and grind my hips to the music, the other two doing the same.

I thrust my hips slow and seductively as if I were fucking someone with deep passion. This causes the girls close by to lean over the stage and start waving a handful of cash while others toss some onto the stage.

I reach up with one hand and loosen my tie, swinging one leg over the chair to straddle it, rocking my hips a few times just before grabbing the chair and lifting it up to place at the end of the stage.

I look out into the crowd and motion with my finger for the closest girl to come up on stage. With little effort, I grab onto her arm and pull her up next to me.

Swaying my hips to the slow rhythm, I pull the knot of my tie until it transforms back into a straight piece of fabric. Grabbing each end, I slide it around her waist and pull her body up against mine, transferring the ends of the tie in one hand. I lean into her neck and grip my hat with one hand while grinding against her, causing her to scream out with excitement.

Out of the corner of my eye, I see Cale and Stone doing the exact same thing. For as little as we actually practice, we're completely in sync with each other. I have to admit we don't look half bad for not putting much effort into the routine.

Walking her backwards, I guide her down into the chair before dropping my tie and ripping the buttons off of my black button down. I grab the girl's hand and place it on my chest while standing above her lap and dancing against her.

The girl's hand goes to reach for my dick, but I grab it, stopping her before she can get there. The thought of another woman touching me there right now is not sitting well with me. It actually pisses me off.

Pushing back my anger, I tilt her chair back until I'm standing over her face, grinding my hips above her while holding the top of the chair up with one hand. My dick is directly in front of her face and all I can think about is Onyx doing something similar with some random dude in her club.

Jealousy courses through me, but I do my best to keep it in check and make it through the dance. The routine is almost over. Only one more thing left to do.

Pulling the chair back up on all fours, I run my hands down my bare chest before undoing my pants and placing the girl's hands on my waistline, allowing her to undress me. She pushes them down my legs without hesitation, leaving me standing here in my short boxer briefs, the women all screaming at us practically naked.

Picking her up and placing her to lie on her back on the stage, I slide across the floor, on my knees, while thrusting my hips until I'm above her face again. I place both hands on the ground in front of me and thrust in a fast motion, brushing against her in the face with my package.

She reaches up and grabs my ass until I'm done and moving down her body, pretending to lick her body on the way down. Once I reach the bottom, I help her to her feet and smile as she shoves a handful of cash in the front of my briefs.

We do a few more short dances, filling the time, until finally the night is almost over and we're heading back stage to get dressed.

I TAKE A SEAT AND look around, swallowing the realization that none of these girls even come close to comparing to Onyx. This place isn't good enough anymore. Onyx is sexy, strong, passionate, and doesn't take shit from anyone. She has always been that way . . . except when it came to me.

I reach over to the table next to me and grab for my beer. I hold it against my lips for a few seconds before pulling it away and setting it down, pissed off at my damn self for thinking. "Fuck me."

"Hello, sexy," a soft voice says from beside me.

Without looking over, I nod my head and reach for my beer again. I really don't feel like being messed with at the moment. "I'm done working for the night," I say stiffly.

"Even better." I feel the couch dip next to me, so I look over to see a sexy brunette. It's the same one that licked the whipped cream off my body that night I left to go find Onyx. She smiles victoriously as if she's been waiting for the exact moment to get me alone. "It looks like you could use some company."

She reaches over and slides her hand up my leg, gripping my thigh just below my dick. I look down at her slender hand and grab it right before she reaches for my package. "I don't want company." I set her hand on her own lap and stand up while taking a sip of my beer. "I'm good being alone."

Leaning forward, she pokes out her chest while running a finger over her half empty glass. Her lips curl up into a smile as she takes a sip and scoots closer to the edge. "I think you just need to release some tension." She licks her lips. "I'm sure I could help you with that."

"I said I'm good." I go to turn around and stop as I almost bump into someone. Not just anyone . . . Onyx.

Her nostrils flare as she stares me in the eyes, not saying a word. I can't even move. I'm frozen in place from her stare, so I just stare back, waiting for her to speak.

"Here's your chance, Hemy." She looks between me and the brunette. "Here's your chance to speak. That is, if you're not too busy."

"Hey!" The brunette sets her drink down on the table next to her and sits straight up as if ready for a fight. "Can't you see he's busy, bitch?"

Onyx runs her tongue over her top teeth before placing the heel of her boot into the girl's chest and shoving her backwards, then leaning down toward her face. "I'd watch who you call a bitch. Got it, sweetheart." She pulls her foot away and leans into her ear. "Keep your dirty little mouth away from my man or you'll be eating my heel for a late night snack."

"Fuck me. That's hot." I set my beer down and watch as Onyx turns around to face me. "Your man, huh?"

"Shit!" She walks away from me while mumbling some shit under her breath.

I quickly catch up to her and grab her by the waist to stop her. "Where are you going?" I spin her around and brush a curl out of her face. "Come to my house with me."

"No." She places her hands on my chest and pushes me away as I pull her into me. "Dammit, Hemy. See what you do to me?" She lets out a breath of frustration and turns away for a second. "I didn't mean to call you that. It just sort of came out."

"It sounded damn good coming out too," I admit. "Come to my house so we can talk. I'm not taking no for an answer anymore."

"No, Hemy. We can talk here. We never talk in private and you know it."

I pull my eyes away from hers and look around to see that a lot of people have stopped to stare at us, including Sarah and one of our other bartenders, Amanda. I flex my jaw at them and they both turn away to resume minding their own business.

"Let's go," I say firmly. "We're going to my house."

"Onyx! What are you doing here?"

I look beside us to see a pretty girl with dark curls standing next to Stone. The look that crosses Onyx's face as she takes her in surprises me. She looks sick, as if she's about to pass out.

"Um . . . Ash. What are you doing here? I thought you were still at work?"

Ash looks between me and Onyx and forces a small smile. "Is this your friend?" She looks me over as if she's trying to figure something out. "The one you said I might meet someday?"

Onyx looks between the two of us, her face pained before she reaches for my arm. "Yeah, but now is not a very good time. I'm suddenly feeling like shit."

Ash steps up beside Onyx and grabs for her purse. "I can take you home. I have my car outside and-"

"No," she cuts in. "You just got here. I'll be fine." She turns to face me and her eyes lock with mine. The pain in her expression confuses me. "Let's go to your house. I think we have a lot to talk about."

"Alright." I take one more look at Stone and Ash before following Onyx through the crowd and outside. As soon as Onyx gets outside, she pukes.

This could be a messy night . . .

CHAPTER THIRTEEN

Hemy

AFTER ONYX CALMED DOWN AND the puking stopped, I took off my shirt and wiped her face off before helping her into my truck. As tough as she thinks she is now, I know she still needs a little taking care of. She deserves it and I want her to know that. I would take care of her for the rest of my damn life if she would just let me.

Onyx lets out a heavy breath beside me. "I can't do this, Hemy. I can't fucking do this. Stop the car."

Pulling the truck over, I grip the steering wheel before slamming my fist into it. I can't stand those words coming from her mouth. I wish she would stop trying to keep me out. "Dammit, Onyx!" I lean back in my seat and rub my hands over my face in frustration. "I've been trying to show you that I'm a different person. Can't you fucking see that? All you want to do is keep me out and push me away."

It's silent for a moment as I stare at the side of her face, taking her in. She looks so pained that it breaks my damn heart. I wish she would just fucking talk and put me out of my misery.

"Hemy," she breathes, breaking the silence. "I know you're trying to prove that you've changed and you can give me what I wanted back then, but you don't understand. You broke me . . . shattered me. I'm not the same girl I was, and I don't think I can love you that way again. You need to let me go. I refuse to go through that again."

Grinding my jaw, I try my best to hide my anger. "You won't even give me the chance, Onyx! I know you're not the same girl and I'm not the same guy. We are different, but that isn't a bad thing. We still belong together like we always have and always will . . ."

She holds her hand up to stop my words before tugging on her hair in frustration. "You know how easy it would be for me to give in and believe you, right? You and I, it's never been easy and I can't go down that path with you, Hemy. Please, leave me alone. Maybe we can be friends someday, but I can't handle this now."

"I can't just be your friend. I'll always want more with you, and you know you feel the same damn way."

She must be done listening to me, because she goes for the door handle and quickly pushes it open. "I'm just going to walk home, and please, don't come after me."

Before I can say anything, she hops out of the truck and slams the door behind her. She takes off walking as if she's trying to get as far away from me as she can. The thought crushes me and I feel as if I can't breathe. I want to be pissed at her for being scared, but I can't. It's my own damn doing and I need to fix this. I knew going in that there was a possibility she wouldn't take me back, but it isn't in me to give up, not this time.

Following her actions, I jump out of the truck and take off after her. I catch up to her quickly, grabbing her arm, and spinning her around to face me. She looks up at me with pained green eyes, before turning away. It's as if looking at me kills her.

"Don't walk away from me when all I've been trying to do is show you how much you mean to me." Wrapping my hands in the back of her hair, I pull her closer to me and force her to look into my eyes. "I fucking love you. Do you know how hard that is for me to say to anyone? Sage is the only other person I have ever said that to and she's fucking gone. You two are the only ones I've ever loved and I lost you both. I want us back. I can't stand to be without you."

"And you don't think I've lost the one person I ever loved? Huh?" She shoves my chest, but I don't budge an inch, which pisses her off more. "Dammit, Hemy!" She shoves me again, but I only hold her tighter, letting her know I'm not going anywhere. I'm not giving up and walking away like she did. Fuck that. I refuse. "I don't love you anymore, okay! I don't want to go back and try again. I won't let history repeat itself. There is no starting over, there is no us, and there never will be. So. Let. Me. Go."

I close my eyes and take a deep breath to calm myself. Her words sting like hell, but I don't believe her for one second. Her eyes give away the truth and that's enough to keep me going. She never was a good liar.

I drug her down into my dark, tormented world of demons and hate, slowly killing her day by day, making it hard for her to breathe. I shook the angel in her and now she's pulling me into her dark, twisted world of hate and revenge, fighting to keep me out, and forcing me to hate her. Well . . . hating her is the last thing I have in store.

"I don't believe you," I say through clenched teeth.

Picking her up, I throw her over my shoulder and hold her up by her ass. She instantly starts struggling against me as I walk her back to my truck.

"Damn you, Hemy! Why are you so hard headed?"

I open the door and shove her inside, being careful not to hurt her. She may want to play games, but I'm going to play harder by showing her the man she fell in love with.

I lean in the window and rub my hands through her hair, causing her to look up at me with a pained expression. She always loved it when I did this in the past. It calmed her down. "You can damn me all you want, but the last thing I'm doing is letting you go again."

Without a word, she swallows and looks away from me. I push back my emotions and walk over to my side of the truck to climb inside. It's time to take her home with me, where she belongs.

She's not leaving until she sees how much I love her . . .

I HATE DOING THIS. I hate trying to push him away when all I really want to do is hold him close and bury my face into his chest. It hurts more than anyone could ever imagine, lying to everyone, even yourself. It's something I have to do now. At first it was just to guard my heart, but now . . . it's because I know he's going to hate me after I tell him what I've been keeping from him for a while now. Why let myself get close and let him in when he'll be hating me soon anyways? I did it for a good reason. I had to.

Hearing him say *I love you* breaks me down, making me want to run into his arms and scream that I love him back, and that I never stopped. Shit, all that will do is guarantee for me to be crushed again. It broke my heart to lie to him and tell him I don't love him anymore. I hate it. I hate it.

Hemy doesn't waste any time driving off, heading in the direction of his street. I can see the fight in him this time. He's different: stronger, sober, and determined, all the things that I hoped for in the beginning. Now . . . it will be me to fuck things up.

I keep my face toward the window for the rest of the ride, fighting my hardest not to cry. I have been strong for four years and I refuse to let anyone see me cry now, especially Hemy. As long as I pretend that I don't have feelings, the safer from him I will be.

When we arrive at his house, Hemy turns to me and reaches out his arm. It's so inviting, making me want to crawl over to him and give into everything I'm fighting. "Come here," he whispers.

I look at him, but don't say a word. I can't or I'll cry.

"I. Said. Come. Here." Reaching over, he pulls me into his lap so that my knees are positioned on the outside of his thighs. "Don't be afraid of me." He wraps both hands in the back of my hair and looks me in the eyes. My heart skips a beat at the warmth of his touch. "I love you more than anything in this world. I would give my life to make you happy. Please, don't be afraid of me. It kills me."

Feeling a tear form in my eye, I try to turn away, but Hemy grabs my face to stop me, his jaw clenching as he watches me.

"Let me see you," he breathes. "I need to see that you still love me. You may not want to say it . . . but I see it. Just let me see it."

I let the tear fall freely down my face, followed by a few more that I can't seem to hold back. Hemy reaches up to wipe my tears away and that's when I lose it. My whole body shakes as I let it all go. All the pain and hurt I have been keeping inside since the day I walked out his door comes raging out.

My face is flooded with tears now. I can barely see Hemy through the mess, but I can feel him squeezing me closer, telling me to let it all out. A part of me feels relieved.

"You're so beautiful," he whispers, while pressing his forehead against mine. "I promise to show you that you're the most beautiful woman in the world to me. Do you understand?"

"Hemy," I cry out. "I need to tell you something. I-"

"Do. You. Understand?" I nod my head, while trying to catch my breath. "I don't want to talk about your doubts or anything bad tonight. I just want to be with you. Can you do that for me? Please."

146

Taking a deep breath, I swallow and wrap my arms around his neck, pulling him as close to me as I can. I love this man so much. He's my world and has been for ten years. This feeling I have right now, in his arms, him holding me as close as he can, is the best feeling in the world and I never want to lose it again.

I feel Hemy plant a few kisses on the top of my head before he reaches for the door and pushes in open.

"Hemy," I cry.

He places both hands on my face and looks at me with questioning eyes.

"I really have something important to tell you tomorrow. This can't wait much longer," I say nervously. "You might just hate me forever after I tell you. I'm so scared."

A small smile crosses his face before he playfully sucks in his lip ring and rubs his thumb under my eye. "Nothing could ever keep me from loving my world and you've been that for the last ten years." He helps me out of his lap and out of the truck before hopping out himself. "Let's go."

Once inside, Hemy runs a bubble bath and lights the candles while I brush my teeth, watching him in the mirror. I still can't get enough of him. I see him approaching me from behind, before I feel his arms wrap around me. I can feel the warmth of his breath kissing my neck.

I lean my neck back and moan as he teases me with his lip ring, running it up my neck and stopping under my ear. "Take your clothes off."

Turning around in his arms, I reach for the bottom of my dress and slowly lift it over my head, with Hemy's strong hands trailing up my skin behind it. His touch gives me instant goose bumps, hardening my nipples, and making my flesh tingle.

Nothing turns me on more than being naked for this man. The way he handles my body is beautiful and breathtaking. He may have a rough exterior, but once he lets you in, he's the best lover you could possibly have; although, this is the gentlest I have ever seen him. It only makes me love him more.

I toss my dress aside. Hemy reaches behind me with one hand and unclasps my bra, before kissing his way down my stomach while pushing down my panties and tossing them aside after I step out of them.

He's standing before me in just his briefs, his muscles flexing as he looks me over. "Undress me, Onyx. This body is yours and yours alone. You'll never have to worry again. I promise."

His words cause me to clench at just the thought of all of this beauty being mine. I hate sharing, especially when it comes to him. I never wanted to, but back then I didn't seem to have a choice.

Getting on my knees, I grip the top of his briefs in my hands and slowly peel them down his muscular body, watching as his cock springs free. Damn, those piercings get me every time. I didn't think it was possible for Hemy to get any more beautiful, but somehow, he has. Everything about his body: his muscles, his tattoos, his piercings, even the way he moves leaves me breathless.

Once I toss his briefs aside, Hemy lifts me up and wraps my legs around his waist, me latching on as he holds me. "Remember what I said to you the last time we were in this tub?"

I nod my head and bite my bottom lip as Hemy steps into the tub and slowly lowers us into the water with me straddling his lap. I have to admit, there is nothing I want more than to have Hemy make love to me. I've wanted it for as long as I can remember and as scared as I am, I need this. I need it so bad.

Gently gripping my waist, he lifts me up before slowly setting me down on his erection, his lips pressed against my neck. We both moan as he eases into me, pushing inside of me as deep as he can fit. Our bodies are plastered together, the both of us holding on for dear life, and it feels so damn good, too good.

Kissing my neck, he whispers, "I love you." He pushes into me while bringing me down to meet his thrust, before whispering again, sending chills up my spine. "Let me hear you say it, Onyx."

He pushes in deeper and wraps me in his arms as tightly as he can. I hold on for dear life, wrapping my legs and arms around him, unable to get close enough. My love for this man is so strong right now that I can barely breathe. I can't hide it anymore. It hurts too damn much.

"I love you, Hemy." He quickens his thrusts, causing me to moan out and grip his hair. "I've never stopped. I can't. I love you so damn much."

He smiles against my lips before crushing his lips against mine and making love to me. Not the rough, crazy sex that I'm used to with him. No, him holding me tenderly and thrusting into me, our bodies both working as one. It's the most intimate moment I have ever shared with Hemy, and it breaks my heart to know that it will probably never happen again.

Tomorrow, I'm going to tear his world apart . . . and mine.

CHAPTER FOURTEEN

Hemy

WAKING UP TO ONYX IN my bed is the best thing that has happened to me in four years. Seeing her here, naked, and wrapped up in my arms is almost enough to make me forget all the bad shit in the world. Almost . . . but not quite. There is still something that's holding me down and as much as I still try to hide the pain, it's always there threatening to surface. I just hope she understands that and tries to be patient. I've grown a lot since four years ago, but I will never be one hundred percent whole.

She stirs in my arms, gripping me tighter as I kiss her on the top of the head. I've been awake for the last hour, but haven't wanted to move in fear of waking her. I'm afraid of what's to come today. She said she had something important to tell me. I have to be honest, it makes me wonder if maybe she has a child with someone that she is afraid to tell me about. I can't stand the thought of that. It kills me.

When I look back down at Onyx, she's looking up at me with a small smile. It makes my heart burst with happiness. Damn, I love this woman. That smile is the best thing to ever happen to me.

"Morning," she whispers. "What time is it?"

I grip a handful of her hair and lean down to crush my lips against hers. She lets out a small moan before smiling against my lips. "It's noon," I respond. "I wanted to let you sleep."

She sits up with a yawn before reaching for her phone. "Crap! I should probably text Ash and let her know that I'm okay. She's probably wondering why I didn't come home last night."

Kissing her one more time, I stand up and reach for my briefs. "Alright. I'll go make us breakfast." I turn back to look at her and smile as she throws on one of my shirts. "Damn, you're sexy as hell in my shirt."

She places her hand on her hip and bites her bottom lip. "You can show me after breakfast."

"Fuck yeah," I growl, while backing away from her and turning into the hallway. Shit, that woman is going to be the death of me.

Opening the fridge, I pull out the eggs and bacon, setting them on the counter. Just as I'm about to reach in the cabinet for some pans, the front door opens. That could only be one person: fucking Stone.

"Don't you fucking knock, asswipe?" I grab out the pans and set them on the stove. This idiot is just lucky that I'm in a good mood for once.

A few seconds later, Stone appears in the kitchen followed by Ash. My eyes linger on her for a moment as she gives me a worried look. There's something about the look in her eyes that seems oddly familiar.

"Is Onyx with you? I haven't heard from her since last night and I didn't know who to ask," she questions while looking around the kitchen. "I called Stone and he said she might be here. Is she?"

Pulling my eyes away, I rub my hands over my face really fast and point down the hall just as Onyx appears.

"Okay, I sent her a text . . ." She looks up to see us all standing in the kitchen and freezes. Her eyes linger over to Ash and she turns ghostly white, all the color draining from her face. "Ash! What are you doing here?"

Ash walks past me and over to Onyx. "What the hell? I was worried sick about you. I'm here to make sure that you're okay."

Onyx leans her head back before turning to face the other direction and breathing heavily. "Shit! I can't do this anymore. I'm so sorry, guys. I'm so damn sorry."

My chest aches from her words. I don't understand why she's so worried about Ash coming here and why the hell she's apologizing to us. I walk towards the girls. "Talk, Onyx. What the hell is-"

I look up and my eyes meet the back of Ash's neck. My whole fucking world comes crashing down in front of me. I have to turn the other way and clench my hands together to keep from breaking something. "Fuck!" I crouch down and grip my hair in anger. This can't be happening. Please tell me Onyx has not been keeping this shit from me. "Onyx. What the fuck? You better start talking and now!"

She's hesitant for a moment, the whole room in a thick silence.

"Ash. I have something to tell you," she whispers. "I have something to tell both you and Hemy. "

Taking a few deep breaths, I stand back up and turn around to face Onyx. I want to see her when she fucking crushes me and turns my world upside down. "Say it," I growl out. "Fucking say it, dammit."

She turns her head away as a tear rolls down her cheek. "God, this is so hard. I never meant to hurt anyone. I just wanted to keep you safe, Ash. Please understand that. I didn't want you to get hurt like I did. I didn't want to get your hopes up and then have your world crushed." She pauses as Ash gives her a confused look. "Back when I met you in that coffee shop in Wisconsin and I saw that scar on the back of your neck . . . I had an idea of who you were."

Ash's eyes widen and her nostrils flare as she rubs a hand over the back of her neck. "What are you saying, Onyx? I don't like where this is going . . ."

Onyx looks over to face the both of us, her face wet with fresh tears. I always hated that look. It fucking hurts. "As soon as you told me you were adopted, I knew you were Hemy's sister. I knew you were Sage. I'm so damn sorry. You're probably going to hate me forever but I did it for a good reason. It's just too bad it's going to hurt us all in the end. Shit," she cries.

Ash lets out a soft breath before turning to face me. Her eyes look pained as she takes me in and shakes her head. My heart fucking hurts as I watch her; my baby sister and she's standing right in front of me.

"That makes no sense. My brother's name was Tyler. His name wasn't Hemy." She looks up at my hair. "And his hair was lighter." She swallows and looks into my eyes. "Those eyes . . ." She turns away.

"Why are you messing with me? Why are you trying to hurt me? Please stop this."

Out of instinct, I step up beside Sage and touch her scar just like I used to when we were kids. Her bottom lip quivers just like in the past and she sucks in a burst of air. It's taking everything in me right now not to break down into tears. I've searched for ten years; ten fucking years, and now here she is, but on top of it Onyx knew and kept it from me. How could she keep something like this from me? Fuck!

"It's the truth, Sage. Shit, I can't believe this is happening." I pause to catch my breath and pull my hand away. "She's telling the truth. You were too young to remember, but I went by my middle name when we were growing up. Dad hated mom for naming me Hemy so everyone started calling me Tyler. It's the only thing you knew me by. That piece of shit. Fuck!" I turn around and punch the wall. "I couldn't fucking find you. I've searched for ten years. I'm so sorry." My voice cracks as I attempt to keep my composure. It's proving to be harder than I thought and all I want to do is ruin my parents and then break down.

Sage lets out a strangled cry before falling down to her knees and covering her face. "This can't be happening. I don't . . ." She sucks in a breath. "I don't know what to say. I've wondered about you my whole life." She shakes her head and cries harder. "Tyler . . ."

Falling down on my knees next to her, I pull her into my arms and press her face into my shoulder as she cries. Holding her next to me makes me want to bawl like a baby, but I fight it. It's so damn hard. I let a few tears fall as the anger and relief floods through me.

I'm relieved to have Sage in my life, but angry as hell that Onyx would do this to me when she knows how badly I've been hurting.

I look up to the sound of Stone's voice. "Holy shit. I'm going to go and give you all some time. I don't need to be here for this. Sorry, man."

I nod my head and pull Sage closer as she wraps her arms around me, her whole body in a shaking mess. "I'm never letting you out of my damn sight again." She lets out something between a cry and a laugh and I can't help but to smile. "I mean that, Sage. Not a day has gone by that I haven't thought about you. I love you so damn much." Her grip on me tightens, but she doesn't say a word. She doesn't have to. It may take her a while to remember me as much as I remember her and that's okay. I'll give her as much time as she needs, but she's not leaving Chicago. Her home is with me, like it should have been over ten years ago.

After what seems like a lifetime, Sage pulls away and looks at my face. She lets one last tear roll down her face before reaching for my hair. "This hair," she says with a laugh. "I think my big brother needs a haircut."

I let out a small laugh and help her up to her feet. I still can't believe she is here and standing in my damn house. The feeling is so surreal.

We both stand here for a moment, taking each other in with smiles before turning to find Onyx pacing around the living room. She's biting her nails and shaking as the tears pour out.

As much as I want to hold her and tell her that it's okay, it really isn't. She just made the worst mistake of her life and it's going to take a while for me to get over this. It doesn't matter what her reasoning is. She hurt me, knowing that she was, and in the worst way possible.

"I'm sorry. I'm so sorry. That's all I can say. You don't think I wanted to tell you? I did. Trust me, I did." Onyx walks over to us and looks between the both of us. "I love you both so much," she cries. "I never meant to hurt anyone, but you have to understand that Hemy is a different person than the one I knew years ago. I couldn't put you through what I had to go through. That's all I can say. I was going to tell you as soon as I knew things were different for real this time." She sucks in a breath and walks past us. "I'm sorry."

"I don't know what to fucking say," I seethe. "I trusted you."

She swallows hard and fights back more tears. "I'm going, just please don't hate me. I can't survive knowing you hate me."

Exhaling, I watch as Onyx walks down the hall and disappears into my bedroom. I'm so fucking mad right now that if I open my mouth again I will probably say something I will regret forever.

So . . . I just watch as she walks away . . . again.

CHAPTER FIFTEEN

Hemy

IT'S BEEN THREE WEEKS SINCE I found out Ash was really Sage and I watched as Onyx walked out of my life again. Not a second has gone by that I haven't thought of her and missed the shit out of her. I have wanted to call her so many times and tell her I forgive her and I understand why she did it, but the pain is still too fresh. As far as I know, she has known about Sage for over a year, over a fucking year. How am I just supposed to forget about that?

A part of me knows that she didn't find me right away because she was scared of getting hurt again and didn't know if she'd be able to handle being around me without losing control, but it hurts like hell. I could have had Sage back in my life that whole damn time. I just can't get over that as much as I want to.

Everything has changed in the last few weeks and besides not having Onyx in my life, things have been good. Sage has been staying with me and I spend most of my time at Mitch's shop instead of at the club. I've told the boys I will stay on for two days a week until they can find someone else to take over. After that, I will stay and bartend. I guess I'm pulling a Slade.

It didn't take long for me and Sage to get comfortable with each other again and we have actually been spending a lot of time together talking about our childhood; only the good stuff though, I'm not reminding her of the all the fucked up shit our parents did to us. She doesn't deserve that and I won't put her through it.

I've been pacing around my living room with a beer in hand for the last three hours, trying to drown out the damn noise in my head. Nothing has been working. "Shit!"

I'm just pulling out another beer when I hear the front door open, so I pull out three beers instead. Sage and Stone have been spending a lot of time together and I need to keep my eye on that slick motherfucker. I won't hesitate to hand him his ass.

"Yo!" Stone calls out while stepping into the kitchen, instantly spotting the three bottles of beer with a grin. "This is why I love you so damn much, man. Always looking out when a brother is thirsty."

I slap him upside the back of the head as he reaches for a beer and pops the top. "Where's Sage?"

He lets out a sigh and quickly takes a drink of his beer. He's hesitant for a moment before he replies. "With Onyx. They've been talking a lot. She's meeting me here in twenty." He takes another drink of beer before setting it down and focusing his attention on me. "That girl loves you, man. I know what she did hurt you, but you have to look at it from her point of view too, man."

I take a gulp of my beer and clench my jaw. "Keep talking." Maybe I need this.

"Alright then. The truth hurts, but . . . from what I've heard, you had a lot of fucking issues. You were never really here." He points to his head and looks me in the eyes. "You can't expect her to risk hurting someone she cares about by bringing them into your sick fucked up world. I know you're not like that anymore, but for someone that experienced it every day for ten years, it's a little harder to convince. You ripped that girl's heart out and stomped on it and she still brought your sister back in hopes that you would be able to meet her one day. She just wanted to make sure the time was right for all of you; not just her, or you, but all three of you. You can't be mad at that, man. That's a good ass woman."

I close my eyes and run my hands through my hair, lost in thought. He's fucking right and hearing someone say it out loud really opens my eyes. She was there for me every fucking time I needed someone.

"You don't have to fucking tell me. She's the best woman I've ever known." I pause to let out a sigh. "I'll never forget that shit."

She's always done what she felt was best. This isn't any different. If I would have gotten Sage back while I was high out of my mind and always fucked up, then I would have probably lost her for good, just like everyone else; her and Onyx. Maybe I can't blame Onyx for being as cautious as she was. Maybe, I should be blaming myself and thanking Onyx. I always was the one to fuck shit up. Still am.

"I fucked up real bad, man. I'm not proud of the things I did one bit. I had a lot of shit I was dealing with and I couldn't handle it without getting out of my head." I open my eyes and grip onto the counter, realizing that I'm the one that fucked up once again. "I need to go find her. Fuck, I can't live without her. I've loved her since the day she attacked me in the alley with a hug. I fell in love with that girl and it took me what seems like an eternity to figure that out. It might be too late now. Fuck me!"

Gripping my shoulder, Stone nods his head in understanding. "Better late than never, asshole," he says jokingly. "Never *too late,* not when you have the kind of love you two have. I have heard it all, man. Now, I'm no mushy pussy or anything, but it's real, bro. Even I can see that."

Shaking off Stone's grip, I pace around the kitchen, trying to get my thoughts in check. I really can't fuck this shit up again. At some point I'm going to be out of chances. No one gives an unlimited supply. I need to let things go and chase after what makes me happy. That has always been her. Always will be.

"I need to go." I rush past Stone and through the living room, slipping on my leather jacket. "Tell me where she lives."

He hesitates.

"Now dammit!"

"Uhh . . ." He closes his eyes in thought for a moment. "1623 Spring Drive." I open the door and get ready to walk out. "Dude, you want me to go with?" he asks.

I turn back around. "Nah. I need to do this alone." I give him a nod. "Thanks, man." Then, I turn around and rush out the door, jumping in my truck.

I'm about two blocks away from Onyx's street when it starts pouring outside. It's coming down so hard that it's making it hard to see out the window. "Fuck! Please be here." I pull up in front of the house and jump out, leaving my truck running. I don't want to waste anymore time being away from her. I can't do it.

I run up to the porch and reach for the handle, but it's locked, so I knock loudly, hoping that Onyx will answer. If it were unlocked then she wouldn't have much of a choice.

A few seconds later the door opens to Sage. She steps out, holding her car keys. "Hey. What are you doing here?" She sounds a little panicked as she looks around. "I'm sorry-"

"It's fine," I cut her off. I don't have time for this right now. "Where is she?"

She shuts the door behind her and holds her hand up in an unsuccessful attempt to block the rain. "I don't know. We were talking and then she just took off on her motorcycle like twenty minutes ago. She seemed upset and in a hurry."

Dammit! I hope she's not caught out in this downpour.

"Fuck!" I punch the porch railing and fist my hair. "I'm going to find her. Where would she be at?"

"I don't know. Maybe at *Vixens'*. She didn't say . . . or maybe at Jade's."

"Alright. I have to go." I grab her head and quickly kiss her on the forehead. "Love you."

"Love you too, Hemy," she screams after me as I run over to my truck and hop in.

Riding around, I start to panic at the thought of Onyx out riding in this weather. Two wheels on slick roadways doesn't mix. I would never forgive myself if something happened to her.

I pull up to *Vixens'* and drive around the whole parking lot in search of my old motorcycle. My heart sinks when I don't spot it anywhere. "Dammit, Onyx! Fuck, you better be at Jade's."

The rain doesn't let up any as I pull back out onto the street and head over to Jade's house. I pull up in front of the house that changed my damn life. If it weren't for Jade's birthday party then who knows when I would have seen Onyx again.

I notice immediately when I pull up that the motorcycle is nowhere to be seen, but I jump out anyway and run through the rain to the door. I knock as hard as I can, losing every bit of patience I have left.

As soon as the door swings open, I rush inside and look around. "Is Onyx here?"

Jade gives me a confused look. "No. What the hell is going on?" She watches me as I run my hand down the front of my face, wiping the rain off. "I haven't talked to her all day."

"Shit!" Without saying another word, I rush back outside and to my truck. Reaching in my pocket, I search for my phone, but come up empty. I must have left it on the kitchen counter at home. "Of fucking course!" I slam my fist into the horn before gripping the steering wheel and letting out an agitated breath. There's only one last place to check and this is a long shot.

Back when we dated, she would surprise me by showing up at Mitch's shop when I was working. She always loved watching me work and I loved having her watch. It was our place. We both made a lot of memories there.

Taking a chance, I head over toward Mitch's shop, looking around for signs of her out on the street, but come up empty. It's already past nine so the shop is closed. Mitch would have left at least an hour ago. That's another reason I have a feeling she's not there either, but I refuse to go home until I look.

When I pull up to the shop, I quickly park and jump out. I look around me, but don't see the bike anywhere. Jogging, I turn around the corner of the building and freeze when I see Onyx standing there in the rain, leaning against the building. She's soaked and more beautiful than if she were dolled up to perfection. The air gets sucked from my lungs at the sight of her and for this moment, I feel more alive than I have in years.

She pushes away from the building and looks at me. "I've been waiting for you," she whispers. One sentence and my heart feels like it's about to burst at the seam.

Well, she'll never have to wait again. That is a promise.

. .

CHAPTER SIXTEEN

Onyx

KEEPING SAGE FROM HEMY WAS the hardest thing I've ever had to do. I just wish he would understand that I did it for Sage, because I love her like a sister myself and was only thinking of her best interests. I could never hurt her in any way. As much as I love Hemy, I had to think of Sage too. Hemy may hate me forever, but I did what I felt I had to do, even though I knew it would end up with him hating me in the end.

I just hope he'll give me a chance to explain, because I don't want to leave here without him. I never want to be without him again. I've lived day after day without him, years on end, and I can't do it anymore.

I've been here for the last half hour or so thinking about us; thinking of all the time we have missed out on and it hurts my heart so bad knowing that I left him and let him down. It kills me. I was scared and young back then. I didn't know what else to do but remove myself from the situation. I should have stuck around and tried to get him help, but I was just a kid trying to deal with something bigger than myself.

I walk closer to Hemy as he stands there in shock and relief, just looking me over as if he can't believe that I'm here. "I was hoping you would come here. I'm so sorry. I wish I could take back what I did, but I can't. You hate me and I don't blame you."

Stepping closer to me, Hemy runs his hands through my wet hair before pressing his forehead to mine, something he always did. "You're wrong," he whispers. "What if I told you I could never hate you, no matter what you do? What if I told you I have loved you since day one, but was too afraid to say it?"

I look up into his eyes and cup his face in my hands. Looking at him makes it hard for me to breathe. The pain I put him through kills me. "How could you even say that, Hemy?" I can't hold my emotions back anymore. Being here in his embrace makes me lose all composure. The tears rush out as I wrap one arm around his neck and hold on for dear life. "I hurt you. I walked out on you when you needed me the most. I never stopped loving you. I thought about you every day and not one day went by that I didn't fear for your life. I was so damn scared."

"I know," he breathes. He rubs both his thumbs under my eyes, wiping the smeared mascara, before cupping my face and hovering his lips above mine. "I was a fool for the way I acted and I should have done the right thing by you. I should have been the one to let you go. I hurt you so damn bad and I'll never forgive myself for what I put you through. You did the right thing. You had to for the both of us, because I was too weak. Watching you walk out of my life and waking up alone is what woke me up. I realized that you were more important than the drugs. No high is better than the high I experience when I'm with you. I'm a different person and I have you to thank for it. Don't ever question what you had to do. Do you hear me?"

His warm breath kisses my lips as he presses his body closer to mine and waits for me to nod. "Hemy," I manage to get out. "I love you so damn much. I'll never-"

Hemy crushes his lips against mine, cutting me off. My body feels weak in his arms as he pulls me as close as possible, kissing me with so much passion that the tears start falling for a whole different reason. I love this man with all my heart and after all that we have been though, I know he feels the same way.

Pulling away from the kiss, Hemy searches my eyes before kissing my tears. "I love you more than life itself. I promise to never hurt you again. All I want is to be with you. I've never wanted anything else besides having Sage back in my life. I have Sage now," he pauses to give me a deep look, his eyes glassing over, "Let me have you. That's all I ask. I need both my girls."

Looking into his eyes makes me weak in the knees. There is so much promise behind them that I know being with him would be different this time. I'm just not sure I can get over me hurting him and Sage. It's myself that I'm angry with now, not him. I'm mad at myself for leaving.

"Are you sure you want me," I ask, my heart pounding.

He kisses me softly before pulling away and smiling. "More than life itself."

We both stand here in the rain just looking each other in the eyes before Hemy sucks in his lip ring and smirks. "Stay here with me tonight. Do you remember those nights?"

I let out a little laugh and nod my head. "How could I forget, Hemy? I can't even count how many people's trucks we had sex in the back of."

"Twenty three," Hemy says with a grin.

I slap his arm. "You kept count?"

He laughs and picks me up, throwing me over his shoulder. "Fuck yeah. Those were twenty-three of the best nights of my life." He bites down into my ass, making me squirm as he pulls out a key and unlocks the door. "I counted a lot of our good memories. Now, tonight will be number one that I undress you out of those wet clothes, put you in my shirt and take care of my future wife. Promise me you'll be mine, forever. Say it. Let me hear you say it."

All the breath leaves my lungs hearing those words leave his lips. I want to cry, but I don't. All I want to do is be close to Hemy and let him back in. No holding back this time.

"I'm yours. Forever," I whisper."

"I've been waiting four years to hear those words," he breathes as he walks us through the dark garage, pulls down the back of a truck bed and carefully sets me down.

He doesn't hesitate undressing himself from his jacket and shirt before pulling off my wet clothes and replacing them with his dry shirt.

He holds me close to him, whispering in my ear and rubbing the back of my head. Here, right now. I feel safe. I feel loved. This is the feeling I want for the rest of my life and can't live without.

It's him and it always has been. Tonight I'm making a promise to never let him go again.

The rest of my life starts tonight . . .

CHAPTER
SEVENTEEN
Hemy

Three weeks later . . .

WE'RE ALL SITTING AROUND IN *Fortune* – a normal
bar, eating dinner and having a few drinks. The whole
crew is here: Slade, Aspen, Cale, Stone, Sage, Onyx and
myself. It's the first time we have all gotten together
since me and Onyx worked things out. I have to admit
it feels good.

It took a bit of convincing, but I finally got Onyx to
move in with me. I knew she would eventually cave in.
The only downfall to that is that it left Sage needing a
new roommate. As you can guess, Stone was quick to
jump to fill that spot. I'm still keeping my eyes on that
slick fucker, but he's grown on me. Plus, he seems to be
crazy about her and she deserves someone to treat her
the way she should have been all along.

"Dude!" I feel something hit me upside the back of
my head. I pull away from kissing Onyx to look over
my shoulder. Slade flicks a chicken wing at me. "Stop

that shit. You're making me want to take Aspen home and fuck her. My cock does not appreciate you right now." Aspen elbows him in the side and laughs. "What?" he questions with a laugh.

"You and your dirty mouth." Aspen grins.

Slade throws his hands up. "My bad." He bends down and kisses her neck before biting it. "You can just punish me later."

"Alright, dicks," Cale says annoyed. "You all can stop your shit now. You're making me sick. I'm trying to eat."

"Shut up and go get your dick sucked, pussy," I say teasingly, causing Cale to toss a fry at my head. What's with the fucking flying food?

Onyx grips my thigh from under the table, causing me to instantly go hard. She always does it, letting me know what she wants. She knows exactly what she's doing to me and as soon as I get her alone, she's getting . . . fucked, and hard.

Aspen smiles over at Cale before taking a sip of her beer. "So . . . Riley gets home next week."

Cale turns white in the face, but quickly tries to shake it off. "Yeah? That's nice," he says, nonchalantly. "Next week, already?"

Aspen laughs and sets her beer down. "Already? It's been like six years since she moved away to Mexico."

I can't even believe how pale and nervous Cale looks. He definitely has it bad for this Riley chick. Maybe he'll man up and finally give his dick up. I knew he was holding back for a reason.

I take a bite of my steak and notice Stone getting a little cozy with my sister at the end of the table. I get ready to say something, but Onyx leans into my ear, distracting me.

"I love you, baby." She places her hand on mine and I smile down at the diamond on her left finger. Knowing that I placed it there makes me the happiest man on earth.

When I proposed to her in the hot tub last week, I about died when she broke down in tears and screamed, *yes*. I'll never forget that feeling for the rest of my life. I'm not going to lie I shed a few tears myself. What can I say? I've waited for a lifetime to have her back in my arms and I'm never letting go. She's my everything. I love her and I love this new life with her. I can't be any happier.

I bite my lip when I realize Onyx distracted me on purpose. I know this now by her little fit of laughter. She saw me eyeing Stone and Sage down. She's good. Too damn good.

When I go to focus my attention on Sage and Stone again; Sage is gone and Stone is chatting with Aspen. That lucky fucker.

I feel a small arm wrap around my neck, distracting me, before Sage rests her head on the top of mine and laughs. "Stop being such a big brother." She squeezes my neck and both girls laugh as Onyx pinches my cheek. "I love you, but seriously . . . don't make me kick your ass. I know what I'm doing with Stone. Okay?"

I look over at Stone and see the look in his eyes as he focuses his attention on Sage as if she's the only woman in the room. I have to respect that. That's the same way I look at Onyx. I need to give Sage the space she needs. I keep forgetting she's a grown woman now.

"Okay," I mumble. "I trust you." She kisses my head and rushes over to sit in Stone's lap, wrapping her arms around his neck. I guess they make a nice couple.

Looking around me; I realize this is the happiest I have ever been in my life. This is where I belong. Where we all belong. This is my family. Family isn't always bound by blood. It's so much more than that. This is it, and it's what I've been missing all along.

I'm ready to spend the rest of my life making my family and future wife happy. This is my ending . . .

The End of #2

Missing Hemy and Onyx already? Be sure to check out the rest of the Walk Of Shame series to get updates on where they stand. This is the order of the series. Also, be sure to check out Hemy's blurb to see what his story is about. Don't miss out. Thank you!

Slade (Walk Of Shame #1)
Hemy (Walk Of Shame #2)
Cale (Walk Of Shame #3)

ACKNOWLEDGEMENTS

FIRST AND FOREMOST, I'D LIKE to say a big thank you to all my loyal readers that have given me support over the last couple years and have encouraged me to continue with my writing. Your words have all inspired me to do what I enjoy and love. Each and every one of you mean a lot to me and I wouldn't be where I am if it weren't for your support and kind words.

I'd also like to thank my special friend, Author of Accepted Fate and editor, Charisse Spiers. She has put a lot of time into helping me put this story together and through this, we have become very close friends. I'm lucky to have her be a part of this journey with me. Please everyone look out for her debut novel Accepted Fate and her upcoming release for July 3rd, Twisting Fate. She has shown me so much support through this whole process and it would be nice to be able to return the favor. Her story is beautifully written and something that the world shouldn't miss out on.

Also, all of my beta readers, both family and friends that have taken the time to read my book and give me pointers throughout this process. My friend Charisse Spiers, Hetty Whitmore Rasmussen. You guys have helped encourage me more than you know. *Bestsellers and Beststellars of Romance* for hosting my cover reveal, blog tour and release day blitz. Hetty has been a big part in making this happen. You all have. Thank you all so much.

I'd like to thank another friend of mine, Clarise Tan from *CT Cover Creations* for creating my cover. You've been wonderful to work with and have helped me in so many ways.

Thank you to my boyfriend, friends and family for understanding my busy schedule and being there to support me through the hardest part. I know it's hard on everyone, and everyone's support means the world to me.

Last but not least, I'd like to thank all of the wonderful book bloggers that have taken the time to support my book and help spread the word. You all do so much for us authors and it is greatly appreciated. I have met so many friends on the way and you guys are never forgotten. You guys rock. Thank you!

ABOUT THE AUTHOR

VICTORIA ASHLEY GREW UP IN Rockford, IL and has had a passion for reading for as long as she can remember. After finding a reading app where it allowed readers to upload their own stories, she gave it a shot and writing became her passion.

She lives for a good romance book with tattooed bad boys that are just highly misunderstood and is not afraid to be caught crying during a good read. When she's not reading or writing about bad boys, you can find her watching her favorite shows such as Sons Of Anarchy, Dexter and True Blood.

She is the author of Wake Up Call and This Regret and is currently working on more works for 2014.

Contact her at:

Facebook:
Victoria Ashley Author and Victoria Ashley-Author

Goodreads:
Victoria Ashley or Slade (Walk Of Shame #1)

Or you can follow Walk Of Shame's Facebook page for more info on the upcoming releases.
Find her other books on Amazon as well.

Other Books by Victoria Ashley

Wake Up Call
This Regret

<u>Walk of Shame</u>
Slade (Walk Of Shame #1)

Made in the USA
Middletown, DE
01 March 2015